TO _____

FROM _____

A new Christmas tradition at our home has begun—a cup of tea, a cozy corner, and a daily reading from *When God Calls the Heart at Christmas*. The short devotions in this book warm my heart. The verses and questions help me pause and reflect on what really matters as we celebrate the most important time of the year. Being a Heartie makes each entry (and the recipes!) feel like a special delight as I connect with other Hearties around the world. I hope this sweet book becomes a new Christmas tradition for you too.

—ROBIN JONES GUNN, author of ninety books,
including the novels that inspired the *Father Christmas* movies
on Hallmark Movies & Mystery channel

When God Calls the Heart at Christmas is a homecoming, a healing spot for rest when you need a reprieve from a world that shouts "Run! Worry! Doubt!" It offers a gentler version of the Christmas season by giving us permission to relax, to enjoy each other, and to take quiet time to wonder at the miracle of the Christ child. You will be blessed by this book!

—KAY MOSER, novelist,
author of the Aspiring Hearts Series

I am a big fan of Brian Bird and Michelle Cox. I've known them for many years and have always looked forward to watching or reading what comes out of their creative minds. Now they join forces in a spectacular way by bringing us into the center of Christmas with stories that will bring joy-filled tears to your eyes, warmth to your heart, and just maybe laughter in your belly!

—BOBBY DOWNES, cofounder of
ChristianCinema.com, A Giving Company

When God Calls the Heart at Christmas is a wonderful mix of touching stories, funny tales, yummy recipes, and biblical truth. I laughed and teared up, longed for the Yuletide Season, and even got a little hungry reading this Christmas treasure. It really is like a Christmas present full of goodies and good cheer. Michelle Cox and Brian

Bird do it once again! Buy this book as a gift for others, but snag one for yourself too.

—SARAH VAN DIEST, author of *God in the Dark:*
31 Devotions to Let the Light Back In

I'm a big fan of *When Calls the Heart* and an even bigger fan of celebrating God. When the two are combined with heartwarming Christmas memories, yummy recipes, and bite-sized messages that stir the soul, I get really excited. Thank you, Michelle Cox and Brian Bird, for the fabulous gift of *When God Calls the Heart at Christmas*!

—TWILA BELK, writer and speaker, author of *The Power*
to Be: Be Still, Be Grateful, Be Strong, Be Courageous

I believe the thread that unites the Hearties is a love for stories that touch the heart. Brian Bird and Michelle Cox have done it again in *When God Calls the Heart at Christmas*. They not only have included the familiar stories from the hit television show, but they've included precious true stories and recipes from the *When Calls the Heart*'s fan base: the Hearties. You can't help but read this one with a smile and maybe a tear or two. This is a Christmas book you'll love year round!

—CAROL HATCHER, writer, speaker

The holidays do not guarantee happiness in every moment for every person. For some, Christmas particularly lends to discouragement, anxiety, fear, and depression. The characters of Hope Valley understand this all too well—but they also know that God can transform our sadness into celebration. *When God Calls the Heart at Christmas* creates more than a place to escape. It provides the hurting with a refuge where they can heal.

—ANITA AGERS BROOKS, inspirational life coach,
international speaker, and award-winning author
of *Getting Through What You Can't Get Over*

FOREWORD BY BEVERLY LEWIS

WHEN GOD CALLS the HEART

at *Christmas*

HEARTFELT DEVOTIONS FROM HOPE VALLEY

Brian Bird & Michelle Cox

BroadStreet
PUBLISHING

BroadStreet Publishing® Group, LLC
Savage, Minnesota, USA
BroadStreetPublishing.com

WHEN GOD CALLS THE HEART AT CHRISTMAS:
Heartfelt Devotions from Hope Valley

978-1-4245-5728-8 (hardcover)
978-1-4245-5729-5 (e-book)

Stock or custom editions of BroadStreet Publishing titles may be purchased
in bulk for educational, business, ministry, fundraising, or sales promotional
use. For information, please email info@broadstreetpublishing.com.

Images from the *When Calls the Heart* series: Copyright © 2018 by Crown Media
Networks, LLC, and used by permission. Other images by Jordan Blackstone:
Copyright © 2018 Jordan Blackstone, and used by permission.

Published in cooperation with the Steve Laube Agency
Cover design by Chris Garborg at garborgdesign.com
Typesetting by Katherine Lloyd at theDESKonline.com

Printed in China

18 19 20 21 22 5 4 3 2 1

This book is dedicated to our precious Janette Oke. Thank you for your faithfulness to God's call on your life. Your "paper missionaries" have literally flown around the world, enriching our lives, touching hearts for God, and giving millions of readers countless hours of enjoyment. Your work has drawn families closer and has been instrumental in bringing our amazing community of Hearties together. We love you more than words can say, and we hope God will continue to bless you abundantly for being such a blessing to all of us.

Thanks be to God
for his inexpressible gift!
2 CORINTHIANS 9:15 ESV

CONTENTS

Whether you're a fan of Hallmark's *When Calls the Heart* TV series or simply can't get enough Christmas, you'll devour *When God Calls the Heart at Christmas*, by Brian Bird and Michelle Cox. This beautifully bound gift book is like a devotional on—well, not steroids—but let's say Christmas cookies! I love the blend of fictional Hope Valley stories set one hundred years ago with the Christmas thoughts and traditions designed for today. The stories, recipes, Bible content, prayers, and spiritual growth questions are perfect for sitting down with the family or reading alone with a cup of hot cocoa.

—KATHY CARLTON WILLIS, God's Grin Gal,
author, speaker

Imagine yourself opening a beautifully wrapped Christmas present only to find it is filled with other beautifully wrapped presents. As you open them, you realize they contain gifts that inspire you, encourage you, or just plain make you feel good. They touch your heart. I felt this way as I opened *When God Calls the Heart at Christmas.* Through devotionals, stories, traditions, recipes, and tales from Hope Valley, this book touched my heart and made me feel good. Thank you, Michelle Cox and Brian Bird, for this beautiful present!

—JOY BROWN, author, speaker, and founder of Words of Joy
and co-founder of Diversified Ministries

Heartie-warming in every way! *When God Calls the Heart at Christmas* is the most marvelous blend of everything we all love about *When Calls the Heart,* with a shining celebration of the Christ of Christmas at the heart of its heart. I'm using this book for a sweet challenge to my own heart this season. Next year too. *Hello, new Christmas tradition!*

—RHONDA RHEA, TV personality, humor columnist,
author of fourteen books, including *Messy to Meaningful,*
Turtles in the Road, and *Fix Her Upper*

*I*s there a better place to spend Christmas than in Hope Valley? Those darling, wide-eyed schoolchildren—Cody, Emily, Anna, and all the others—counting the hours until Christmas morning dawns with all its festivities, fun, and joy of family and friends. Elizabeth's list-making and gift-gathering are at last complete as she and her adoring Jack—with his winning smile—celebrate their love and God's great love in sending the most precious of all gifts: the Christ child.

To my husband, Dave, and I, Elizabeth, Jack, and the extraordinary cast of *When Calls the Heart* have become like extended family, finding their way deep into our hearts.

When we began watching these wonderful characters, I immediately found myself connecting with Elizabeth Thatcher during the pilot episode and then into the first season. I tried to imagine what each new season might bring her way, and I was captured by her love of journal writing, school teaching ... and Christmas-keeping. I was swept up in her hopes and dreams, cheering her on in every episode. She endeared herself to me by going out of her way for those less fortunate, hurting, or left out, all in the midst of her own homesickness for her family and everything she had loved and left behind for this new calling in Hope Valley. Truly, Elizabeth lives her life as though loving others matters.

At Christmastime we dust off our manners, don't we? Or do we? Are we actually willing to emulate Abigail Stanton's forgiving spirit toward Henry Gowen at Christmas ... and every day? Or, maybe we could benefit from a "kindness week" like the one Elizabeth assigns her young students. What if we simply befriended someone who seemingly doesn't belong? And really, why wait till Christmas to embrace the Golden Rule?

Another favorite character of mine is Lee Coulter—so measured and wise with that ever-present twinkle in his eyes. I love his understated humor and his near-fatherly way with Cody. Remember the heartwarming scene where Lee seeks Cody out and takes him under his wing to simply play a round of catch? And Cody's surprise when Lee gives him the autographed softball! One is a tangible gift, and one is a heart-gift—the gift of making time for a lonely child. You and I know that Lee has a heart of gold, and he never hesitates to spread thoughtfulness around Hope Valley. What if we mimicked those same beautiful qualities every season of the year?

My longtime friend Brian Bird is a man of similar qualities. In fact, I cannot think of a more fitting author for this wonderful devotional because Brian's vision for stories that lift the spirit and make a difference in our world are so evident in all of his movies and books. We are all incredibly grateful to "Papa Heartie" for his vision for this amazing series.

As for Hope Valley at Christmastime, it's not only the idyllic and historic setting we've come to love—the fresh and glistening snowfall, the jingle of sleigh bells, the aroma of Abigail's apple cobbler—but it's also an attitude, an approach to life. For millions of viewers it's a throwback to the way our grandparents lived with integrity and purpose, embracing the simple gifts of honesty, patience, respect, faith, family, and generosity.

So I welcome you to open your heart and come home to Christmas right here within the delightful pages of this most heartwarming and inspiring book.

—Beverly Lewis, *New York Times* best-selling author

CELEBRATE CHRISTMAS
IN HOPE VALLEY

*C*hristmas truly is the most wonderful time of the year. Whether it's in the fictional town of Hope Valley in the early 1900s, or in our lives today, there is nothing more profound than celebrating God's most important gift to the world. If ever there was a time to celebrate, this is it.

That's what *When God Calls the Heart at Christmas* is all about—a celebration of faith, food, family, and the most meaningful Yuletide traditions. It's a big birthday party for God!

We know time is often in short supply at Christmas so we've kept the offerings in this book in manageable sizes. First up in each chapter is a devotional to set the tone for your day— and you'll find God-moments that we discovered in Hope Valley at Christmas. After that, we'll share a verse, a prayer, and some questions ("The Gift of Your Heart") to help you discover a deeper relationship with God this Christmas.

Following each devotional is a holiday recipe you and your family can enjoy together—and they're especially awe- some because many have come from the kitchens of Hearties around the world. Let your children help you with these recipes and make some extra sweet memories this Christmas.

Next, you'll discover Christmas stories and traditions—some funny and some poignant—to make your family celebration even more special. Many of them were also shared by Hearties.

So we hope you'll journey with us to Hope Valley as we focus on all the reasons for this most blessed season—because as shepherds, angels, and wise men learned on that holy night so long ago—when God calls your heart at Christmas, you can expect a celebration.

By Jordan Blackstone

WHAT IS YOUR
UNEXPECTED STORM?

We usually associate Christmastime with happiness, but for Jack and Elizabeth, the joy was tempered the year he came home unexpectedly. He was overjoyed to be back for a few days with Elizabeth, but knowing he'd have to return to the Northwest Territories before Christmas Day left a cloud over them both.

Abigail had been excited to have Becky coming home for Christmas—their first official Yuletide as a family. She was devastated when the telegram arrived with news that a snow-storm had stranded Becky in Nelson Ridge. Her heart was broken, but worse, how would she tell Cody? He'd been so excited his sister was coming home.

As most of us discover sooner or later, there are unexpected heartaches that come at us rain or shine, sometimes even at Christmas. Maybe it's a financial situation that makes the gifts under your tree skimpy or even nonexistent. Or perhaps you've suffered the loss of a loved one, a broken relationship, or a health problem.

Those times can prove difficult, but they can also be blessings in disguise because they cause us to lean on God in ways we wouldn't otherwise. And sometimes the same storms that bring challenges can also be surprise godsends. The storm Becky needed to be rescued from was the same storm that allowed Jack to stay home an extra few days. That's the way God works. When life brings unexpected change, we can expect one thing from Him: He *never* changes.

Not only so, but we also glory in our sufferings,
because we know that suffering produces
perseverance; perseverance, character;
and character, hope.

ROMANS 5:3–4 NIV

Dear Lord, I don't like disappointments and difficult circumstances—especially at Christmas. Even though my heart is heavy, remind me of why we celebrate this time each year, of the joy of your amazing gift of ultimate love and redemption for the world. Help this hard time to draw me closer to you. Help me to feel your presence in a special way. Thank you for always being with me and for the comfort you bring. Amen.

THE GIFT OF YOUR HEART

* **How can difficult times actually be blessings?**
* **How should you respond when those difficult moments come into your life?**

From the Kitchen of Heartie Marnie Swedberg

INGREDIENTS

Brownie Layer

    Your favorite boxed brownie mix, made as directed
    1 teaspoon peppermint extract

Middle Layer

    2 cups powdered sugar
    1/2 cup softened butter
    1 tablespoon water
    1 teaspoon peppermint extract
    3 drops green food coloring

Top

    1 cup semi-sweet chocolate chips
    8 tablespoons butter
    1 teaspoon peppermint extract

PREPARATION

Preheat the oven to 350 degrees. For the brownie layer, use your favorite boxed brownie mix. Make as directed on the box and add one teaspoon of peppermint extract. Mix well and then pour the mixture into a greased 13x9x2 pan. Bake for 30 minutes or until a toothpick inserted near the center comes out clean.

For the middle layer, mix together the two cups of powdered sugar, the half cup of softened butter, the tablespoon of water, the teaspoon of peppermint extract, and the three drops of green food coloring; blend until smooth. Layer onto the cooled brownies.

For the top layer, melt the cup of semi-sweet chocolate chips, eight tablespoons of butter, and the teaspoon of peppermint extract. Stir until smooth. Spread over the green layer.

THIS TREE WAS MEANT FOR YOU

From Heartie Dee Dee Baxter Parker
(As Told to Michelle Cox)

*M*y beautiful daughter, Brooke, had fought for several years against the cancer that had invaded her body, but it had taken a heavy toll on her. As Christmas Eve night arrived, she was quite weak, propped on pillows on the couch, her head bald from the effects of the chemo and radiation.

Brooke had always loved Christmas, but this year, her husband and I had been so busy caring for her that Christmas decorations had been the last thing on our minds. But as she looked around the room that night, Brooke said softly, "I wish we had a Christmas tree."

In our hearts, we knew this might be her last Christmas, and we wished we'd put a tree up for her—but it was the night of Christmas Eve and I figured it was too late to go get one, and besides, money was tight because of all the medical bills. But then her husband remembered seeing an artificial tree propped in a corner of the attic, one that had been left by the previous owners.

He ran to the attic to get it, but when we set the tree up in the room, it was beyond pitiful. The tree listed to one side, and there were holes where limbs were missing. With her beautiful smile, Brooke said, "We can put tinsel on it and it will fill in the blank spaces and be pretty." We tried, but it still looked horrible.

The weather was bad that night, so I was a little surprised when Brooke's husband said he needed to go out. We thought he went to get milk, but he was gone for so long that we were getting worried.

But as the grandfather clock chimed ten o'clock, he walked in carrying the most gorgeous Balsam fir Christmas tree you've ever seen. He'd known it was a long-shot for any of the tree lots to still be open, much less have any pretty trees left, but he drove into one of the lots anyway.

The owner of the lot was closing up, but this husband-on-a-mission went ahead and asked if he still had any trees, explaining about how sick his wife was and her desire for a Christmas tree.

The man said, "Son, come on around back."

When they got behind the lean-to, the lot owner explained that a lady had paid for a tree and told him, "You'll know when it's the right person."

He'd gotten worried as days went by and nobody had come that fit that description. He said, "Now I know this tree was meant for you."

That night Brooke put the hooks on the ornaments and we decorated the tree, laughing together and making memories to last a lifetime. It was a lovely time.

Many Christmases have passed since then, but I'll always be grateful for that miraculous Christmas when a generous, foresighted lady's kindness provided my beloved daughter with the perfect Christmas tree.

THE CHRISTMAS PRESENT
THAT NEVER DISAPPOINTS

By Jordan Blackstone

*L*ee Coulter wanted to do something special for his wife, Rosemary, for their first Christmas as husband and wife. Knowing of her love for baubles, he bought her a unique brooch for her Christmas gift—one he thought would tickle her fancy.

Lee also knew of her penchant for snooping, so he hid the gift in a place she'd never look. But ever-vigilant Rosemary spied it out anyway—and let's just say she wasn't excited about her new accessory. "Horrified" might be a better word.

It's easy to chuckle at fictional characters who have over-the-top reactions to poorly chosen gifts—but what do you do when you receive a gift that disappoints you? Or when you open a package that isn't what you hoped for—such as that hideous sweater from grandma?

The good news is that God's gifts never disappoint. One of His best gifts is the people in our lives who love us. They may offer us presents that either delight or displease, but the real present is their presence. What better blessing is there than knowing we can have deep, meaningful relationships with family and friends, no matter what their taste is in gift-giving.

God has put those people in our lives as a preview of His greatest gift: His beloved Son sent to the earth to bring us peace, joy, purpose, and salvation. And when you open that gift, not only will it never disappoint … it will change your whole world.

Every good and perfect gift is from above,
coming down from the Father of the heavenly lights,
who does not change like shifting shadows.

JAMES 1:17 NIV

*Lord, for Christmas this year, please give me a thankful
heart. Help me to be grateful for all the gifts in my life,
whether they be people, presents, or purposes you have for
me, and thank you for accepting the sometimes pitiful gifts
I bring to you. Help me to have the same graciousness for
others that you have for me. Amen.*

THE GIFT OF YOUR HEART

* **Why are meaningful relationships with family
  and friends such a special gift?**

* **How would our relationships change if we were
  as gracious to others as God is to us?**

MINI PEPPERONI CHRISTMAS TREE PIZZAS

From the Kitchen of Heartie Laurel Leidy-Cox

Sometimes when we plan our holiday menus for parties and family get-togethers, we forget about having foods that the children will enjoy. These are always a favorite with the little ones—and with the kids-at-heart as well.

INGREDIENTS

A bag of frozen yeast roll dough
A jar of pizza sauce
A bag of mozzarella cheese
A bag of mini pepperoni pieces

PREPARATION

Use one frozen roll for each mini pizza. Place on a cookie sheet that has been sprayed with cooking spray, leaving room for the dough as it rises and spreads. Heat the oven to about 170 degrees and then turn it off. Sit the dough in there to rise. This will take three to five hours or until it's doubled in size.

Pat the dough into a circle with your hands until it reaches the size of a mini pizza (approximately five inches across). Spread pizza sauce onto the dough. Top with mozzarella cheese, and then add the mini pepperoni pieces, shaping them into a simple Christmas tree shape.

Bake at 425 degrees for about seven to eight minutes or until the dough is lightly browned and the cheese is melted.

The Christmas Snoop

From Heartie Michelle Cox

R osemary Coulter wasn't the only snoop at Christmas. My youngest son, Jason, seemed to excel at that, so I always tried to wrap his gifts before he got home from school because I knew he'd find them if I didn't do that.

So one year as he opened his Christmas gifts, my mama radar kicked on. How could he know that was his Carolina basketball jacket *before* he opened the present? As he tore wrapping paper from the next two or three boxes, I overheard him make comments like, "This must be my __." Or "I bet this is my __."

Finally, I said, "Okay, young man. You're busted. I wrapped those gifts before you had a chance to see them, so how do you know what's in all those boxes?"

With a sheepish look, he explained, "Well, I discovered that if I slit the tape and squeezed the box, it would pop open far enough that I could see what was inside. And then I taped the box back."

Let's just say that duct tape might have been involved in wrapping his gifts the next year.

But that wasn't the end of Mr. Christmas Snoop. The next year rolled around, and as usual, Jason spent hours snooping for his presents. He searched the closets, made his rounds through the basement, looked in dresser drawers, and even checked frequently in the trunk of the car to see if any gifts were there. The kid could have probably done inventory for our house.

Jason had asked for a much-desired electronic game for Christmas, so I suspected he'd be even more diligent about searching for his gifts. I was right.

I wracked my brain for the perfect place to hide his present, and then in a moment of pure genius, it came to me. I wrapped his game and put it in the one place I knew Jason would probably never look—and certainly wouldn't clean without being forced—I hid it under his bed.

Despite all his searching, he didn't find it. On Christmas morning after he opened his prized gift, he said, "Where did you hide it? I looked everywhere!"

I quietly replied, "I hid it under your bed."

He said, "No, seriously, where did you hide it?"

Trying to hide a grin, I replied again, "I hid it under your bed."

Yes, folks, all those weeks of unsuccessful searching, and he'd been within a few feet of his gift the whole time. And that's how I accomplished one of my greatest mom moments ever. Don't you think there should be a Christmas trophy for that?

❀ 3 ❀

THEIR PAIN ...
IN YOUR HEART

*S*adness isn't an emotion we typically think of at Christmas, but it's something that many people experience during the holidays—whether from the loss of a loved one, a serious illness, being alone, or struggling financially.

Hope Valley's Myra McCormick was one of those people. Her husband's death had plunged her into deep depression. Christmas cheer didn't exist in her cabin, and her bitterness caused her to push people away. That is, until Dr. Carson

Shepherd came on a house-call. He looked beyond her bristly personality and saw her wounded soul. Compassion welled up in him, and he set his heart on bringing some Christmas joy to Mrs. McCormick.

His task wasn't easy. She declined the decorations he offered for her cabin. When he took a wagonload of children to sing Christmas carols, she shut the door on them—but he didn't quit, because helping her was the Yuletide thing to do.

Are there people in your life who are hurting this Christmas? What could you do to bring the joy of that little manger in Bethlehem into their lives? How could you demonstrate that they are loved by you … and by the Father who loves them first, most, and best of all?

Don't let the Scrooges in your life keep you from practicing compassion. Having empathy is cultivating their pain … in your heart. Let compassion for others be the gift you open up not just at Christmas, but every day of your life.

Bear one another's burdens,
and so fulfill the law of Christ.

GALATIANS 6:2 NKJV

Dear Father, please give me a heart of compassion. Let me see others through your eyes and help me look beyond their exterior and see their hearts. Help me to love even when it's unwarranted ... just as you always do for me. Send someone to me this Christmas who needs to hear about you. Show me how to bear their burdens with them so I can lighten their load. Fill their hearts with the joy of Christmas. Amen.

THE GIFT OF YOUR HEART

* **What specific things can you do this Christmas to help someone who is hurting?**

* **How does it help us to care about difficult people if we see them through God's eyes?**

TWICE-BAKED POTATO CASSEROLE

From the Kitchen of Heartie Michelle Cox

INGREDIENTS

8 average-size potatoes
6 tablespoons butter
1/2 cup sour cream
Salt, to taste
2 teaspoons chives
2 cups cheddar cheese, divided
4 strips of cooked bacon, optional

PREPARATION

Wash, peel, and cube the potatoes. Cook them in boiling water until tender; drain well. Mash the potatoes until fluffy. Add the butter, sour cream, salt, chives, and 1 1/2 cups of the cheddar cheese; mix well. If the potatoes seem dry, you can add a little milk.

Place into a greased baking dish. Bake at 350 degrees for about 20-30 minutes or until the potatoes are hot and slightly browned. Remove from the oven. Top with the remaining 1/2 cup of cheese and place the casserole back in the oven until the cheese has melted. Top with crumbled bacon if desired.

STOCKINGS FILLED
WITH LOVE

From Heartie Martie Noll

When I was home from college one Christmas, I visited a friend's mother in the hospital. Afterwards I wandered around and ended up in the children's wing. I was sad to see so many there just a few days before Christmas.

Later, I told my mother of my sadness for these children. As she listened, I watched her get out her old Singer sewing machine. She turned to me with a twinkle in her eye and said, "Come on, let's get to work. We are going to make those children smile." She pulled out some red felt and other odds and ends, and we decided to make them all a stocking. Each one was different with decorations of glitter, sequins, and any felt design we could create. When we were done, we filled each stocking with candy.

Christmas Eve night I gathered up all the stockings and went back to the hospital. I checked with the surprised nurse to see if it was okay to pass out my little stockings. After her approval, I walked quietly down the hall.

I was nervous going into my first room but the little girl smiled broadly when she saw me. I showed her a stocking. As I looked around, I noted that she had a father there who was busy watching TV. She seemed so alone. We talked and laughed for a little while before it was time for me to move on.

I went from room to room passing out my little red stockings. I wished they had something more in them. They seemed so small and insignificant. Yet, I marveled at how excited each child was to receive one. I realized they were filled with something more than candy. They were filled with love, care, and hope. Even a little child could sense those feelings.

Finally, I went to the last room. I was tired and had planned to make a quick stop before I headed home. Inside I found a little blonde boy about six years old, sitting alone, looking out the window. When he heard me, he gave a small smile then continued looking out into the night. How could he be all alone on Christmas night? My heart hurt for him.

I spent some time with him, playing a game we made up and singing Christmas songs. As I finally had to leave, I handed him the little red stocking. It was only about seven inches long, but he acted like it was huge. He gave it a hug and then gave me one.

Walking to my car that night, it felt like I had just experienced the true beauty of Christmas.

Years later, I began working in hospital ministry, and did that for ten years. Now I'm in my eleventh year in bereavement ministry. My mother had taught me how to be creative in giving to others. God taught me the importance of walking alongside the hurting.

Yes, that Christmas evening impacted my life forever.

4

SCONES OF
HUMAN KINDNESS

With the heartache that Henry Gowen had always brought to Abigail Stanton's family and to Hope Valley (not to mention his less-than-delightful personality), Abigail could have been forgiven for having hard feelings. She could have focused on all of Henry's bad traits, but instead, she looked for the good in him.

And she demonstrated her character at Christmas when she reacted to Henry with unexpected kindness. Instead of gifting him with what he deserved, she baked some of her special scones and sent the gift to Henry at the federal detention center in Cape Fullerton, where he was being held for stealing town money.

We often find ourselves surrounded by family, friends, and co-workers at Christmas—and sometimes, they're people who've hurt us. When that happens, it's easy to want to avoid them, right? But what if, like Abigail, we asked God to help us look for the good in them? Even better, what if we asked Him to point out the hurt feelings in our own hearts as a way of helping us empathize with the unlovable aspects of others? After all, isn't that exactly what God does for us? He looks beyond our faults and failures and loves us anyway.

Friends, who's the Henry Gowen in your life? What scones of kindness can you offer that person this Christmas? You see, bitterness doesn't hurt others—it hurts us—but acts of kindness and forgiveness are usually the cure for what ails everybody. Time to get baking!

Love is patient, love is kind. It does not envy, it
does not boast, it is not proud. It does not dishonor
others, it is not self-seeking, it is not easily angered,
it keeps no record of wrongs.

1 CORINTHIANS 13:4–5 NIV

*Dear Lord, why is it sometimes so hard to be kind to
others—especially when they're difficult to be around or
they've hurt me or someone I love? Please show me where I
have wrong feelings towards family, friends, or co-workers.
Help me to look for the good in others, even when I have
to work hard to find that. Instead of repaying what they
deserve, help me to extend the grace and forgiveness that
you've shown to me. Amen.*

THE GIFT OF YOUR HEART

* Who's the Henry Gowen in your life? How can
  you show kindness to that person—even though
  it's unmerited?

* How can you extend the grace and forgiveness
  that God has shown to you?

DEB'S CINNAMON SCONES

From the Kitchen of Heartie Deborah Raney

INGREDIENTS

- 2 1/4 cups all-purpose flour
- 1 teaspoon salt
- 1 1/2 teaspoons baking powder
- 1/2 teaspoon baking soda
- 1/2 cup white sugar
- 2 teaspoons cinnamon
- 1/2 cup (1 stick) cold butter, cut in cubes
- 1 cup sour milk or sour half-and-half (you can sour milk by adding 2 tablespoons vinegar per cup of milk)

Topping

- 1 egg, well-beaten
- 1/2 cup cinnamon sugar mixture (about 5 parts sugar to 1 part cinnamon)

Icing

- 1 cup powdered sugar
- 2 tablespoons butter, softened
- 2 tablespoons half-and-half or liquid coffee creamer
- 1 teaspoon vanilla

PREPARATION

Preheat the oven to 425 degrees. Sift together the flour, salt, baking powder, baking soda, sugar, and cinnamon. Cut the butter into the dry ingredients with a pastry cutter until the mixture is like fine bread crumbs. (Tip: Since keeping the butter cold while preparing this is important, it's helpful to get everything ready before you cut the butter into the flour mixture.) Add the buttermilk. Stir quickly with a fork until the dough forms a ball.

Dust your hands with flour and turn the dough onto a floured board. Knead gently about ten times, working in a small amount of additional flour. Flatten the dough into a one-inch thick circle. (It will be about 12–15 inches in diameter.)

Paint the circle of dough with the beaten egg (depending on the size of the egg, it may only take half). Then sprinkle the cinnamon sugar mixture evenly over the top of the dough circle. Using a pizza cutter or sharp knife, slice dough pizza-style into twelve equal triangles. Transfer to a greased cookie sheet, leaving half an inch between the scones. Bake for 12–15 minutes at 425 degrees. The scones are done when they have a light golden color. Cool.

For the icing, mix the powdered sugar, softened butter, half-and-half, and vanilla until blended and smooth. Drizzle the cooled scones with the icing.

THE CHRISTMAS BIBLE

From Heartie Stacey Mathews

I never fully understood what Christmas was truly about until I reached my mid-teens. When I was about fifteen I started attending church with my best friend. Her father was the pastor. My friend, LuAnn, had a Bible and she would whip through the pages quickly while her father preached every Sunday. I spent most of my church time sharing LuAnn's Bible and learning about Christ.

During Thanksgiving at our annual family gathering, various relatives asked what us kids wanted for Christmas. I quietly said, "A Bible."

On Christmas Eve, we exchanged gifts. I was disappointed that I didn't receive a Bible—but I knew it was a rough time for my family due to job layoffs. Then on Christmas Day, I discovered a present wrapped in shiny red paper. When I opened the gift, I saw a black cover with gold lettering and the words, "Holy Bible." I was so happy to see that it was the Bible I'd requested. It became my constant companion at church and at home.

That Bible is decades old now. The pages are yellowed and worn from years of use—but I've never forgotten the kindness of my relative in giving that Bible to me, and I know without a doubt that it's the best Christmas gift I ever received.

A PROGRESSIVE CHRISTMAS

From Heartie Bobbi Schutte

Christmas Day was so special when I was growing up. My mom had seven brothers and sisters, and the families all went from home to home on Christmas Day, ending at our house. It was like a progressive dinner concept but with each family sharing their specialty food and Christmas cookies.

You can imagine how many people that was going from home to home, and some of the homes were very small. But that made it all the more special. We were together enjoying the beauty of Christmas. The women would share their food and cookies, and they'd gather around and show the other ladies and girls what they received for Christmas.

The men and boys would watch sports or show off their new guy stuff. And the kids would go wherever there was free space—the basement, attic, bedrooms, or backyard, depending on the weather. We often had snow, so we were inside most years. Needless to say, the kids loved to spend time simply jumping on the beds together.

I'm so thankful for those memories, and I've continued that tradition with my own family for many years. That's likely one of the reasons I'm drawn to *When Calls the Heart*—I see the Hope Valley families come together for Christmas and other special events. The kindness and love found there are reflected in my own family. What a beautiful gift to behold and treasure— and what precious memories to tuck away forever in my heart.

⚜ 5 ⚜

COME HOME

*E*lizabeth Thatcher missed Jack Thornton while he was away fighting outlaws. His cause was important, but watching him ride away from Hope Valley had shattered her heart. A day didn't go by that she didn't miss him. With every breath. On every new morning. At every sunset.

The longing was even deeper with Christmas drawing near. Of course she wanted Jack home to have someone to celebrate with as Hope Valley prepared for a parade and fulfilled wishes left on the Christmas Wishing Tree. But most of all, she just wanted him back safe and sound, in her arms where he belonged. She felt that half of her heart was missing—and there was no cure except for Jack.

You know what? God misses us. His heart breaks whenever we walk away from Him or when life distracts us from our relationship with Him. He loves sweet fellowship with us. He longs for our voices as we kneel and talk to Him, and He misses us listening as He whispers to our souls.

The God who made the universe—who loves the world so much that He sent His Son to sacrifice Himself for our wrongs—cares about the smallest details of our lives. It boggles the mind, but it's true. And the only cure for God missing us is for us to come home. Do you need to come home to God today? A warm welcome is waiting for you and it would be the perfect Christmas gift to Him.

Return to the LORD your God,
for he is gracious and compassionate,
slow to anger and abounding in love.

JOEL 2:13B NIV

Dear Lord, I know I must test your patience when I wander and stray from your will for my life. I'm sorry that I brought distance between us and that I sometimes reject you. I'm so grateful that you love me enough to always welcome me home—that you're waiting for me with open arms. Help me to feel your presence and to draw closer to you. Amen.

THE GIFT OF YOUR HEART

* **How do you think God feels when you are distant from Him?**

* **How does it affect you to know that God cares about the little details of your life?**

GRANNY COLE'S 4-FLAVOR HALF POUND CAKE

From the Kitchen of Heartie Minnie Woody

This cake has been a family favorite for about fifty years. It's easy to make and always turns out well.

INGREDIENTS

2 sticks butter (no substitutions), softened

2 cups sugar

5 eggs

Pinch of salt

2 cups all-purpose flour

1 teaspoon vanilla

1 teaspoon almond flavoring

1 teaspoon coconut extract

1 teaspoon butter flavoring

PREPARATION

Do not preheat the oven. Cream the butter and sugar until fluffy and blended. Add the eggs one at a time; beat well after each addition. Combine the salt and flour and add it slowly to the butter mixture.

Turn the mixer to low and add the vanilla, almond flavoring, coconut extract, and butter flavoring. Mix well and then pour into a tube pan that has been greased and floured. Bake at 325 degrees for about one hour. (Start in a cold oven.) Don't open the oven door until the time is up. The cake is done when golden brown and when a knife inserted in the middle comes out clean.

Always Leave
One Christmas Gift
for Later

From Heartie Patty Bird

*C*hristmas sometimes is as much about the journey as it is the destination. The anticipation of holidays—all the preparation, the shopping, the baking and get-togethers—can be just as much fun as the actual day itself. But because of that big build up, the week after Christmas can be a huge downer. It's no wonder we hear stories of letdown and depression in the days following the festivities.

That's why in the Bird family, one of the fun traditions that always seems to be a hit with our kids—and now with our extended family through marriage—is our custom of saving one surprise group gift for the week after Christmas. And each year, my husband, Brian, and I try to outdo ourselves in the planning.

Examples have included a trip to *Cirque du Soleil*, a nighttime ride on a Christmas train through the old mining town of Georgetown, Colorado, a mystery dinner theater, complete with the rubber chicken supper and cheesy comedy, and a visit to an escape room, where the whole family was locked in a mystery-themed maze of rooms and we had to work together to solve a series of riddles and puzzles within an hour to unlock the door. We made it out of our escape room experience with just a minute to spare.

The tradition has actually become one of my favorite parts of Christmas. In our increasingly busy world—and now that our kids are almost all grown and gone—we miss them being home all the time. Just stopping to spend time with our brood means the world to Brian and me ... even if it means listening to lame jokes at a dinner theatre.

6

THE GIFT THAT
GIVES BACK DOUBLE

Snow swirled through the air, carried by frigid gusts of
wind. Times were already hard in the tent settlement near
Hope Valley, but with winter's arrival, life was even harsher.
The bleak weather matched the spirits of the settlers as Christmas approached. The tents usually provided some shelter, but
each blast of wind felt like it blew straight to their bones. They
hadn't felt warm in days.

They were excited about getting permanent residences,
but that was scant comfort in the midst of daily misery. So you

can imagine their relief when Pastor Frank and Nurse Faith arrived with news that the townsfolk had invited the settlers to stay with them until their homes were ready—an early Christmas gift.

Put yourself in the shoes of Hope Valley's citizens. Having families move in with them at Christmas was undoubtedly inconvenient. But they did it because that's what people of faith do. We hold out open hands to the homeless, the friendless, the disenfranchised, and sometimes, even the stranger.

For those who have no experience with church or the Bible, people of faith may be the only example of true hospitality they will ever see. A warm meal. Shelter from the cold. A helping hand. It doesn't sound like much, but when we give willingly, the impact can be soul-transforming. And here's a secret: When we extend generosity to others, we always end up blessed as well, because hospitality is the gift that always gives back double.

Show hospitality to one another
without grumbling.

I Peter 4:9 esv

Dear Lord, give me a tender spirit that will be touched by the heartache and needs of others, and help me to go the extra mile without complaint. Help me to love those who seem impossible to love. Make my home a place where people will feel a warm welcome, where their hearts will heal and where they will sense your presence in every room. Amen.

THE GIFT OF YOUR HEART

✳ How does it affect you to realize that you might be the only example of God's love that someone might ever see?

✳ How does it transform you personally when you extend generosity or kindness to others?

NANNY'S SUGAR COOKIES

From the Kitchen of Rita Lawter

This recipe has been in our family for fifty years. We made these cut-out cookies every year when our sons were little. Then when the grandchildren came along, we would gather around the island in the kitchen and bake and decorate the cookies. Now we're continuing the tradition each year with our great-grandchildren.

INGREDIENTS

> 1/2 cup butter
> 1 cup sugar
> 1 large egg
> 1/2 teaspoon vanilla
> 2 to 2 1/4 cups all-purpose flour
> 2 teaspoons baking powder
> 1/2 teaspoon salt

Glaze

> 1 cup powdered sugar
> 5–6 teaspoons of water
> Food coloring, optional

PREPARATION

Preheat the oven to 375 degrees. Cream the butter, sugar, egg, and vanilla; blend well. Sift the flour, baking powder, and salt together and blend into the creamed mixture. Divide the dough in half. Chill for one to two hours so the dough will be easier to handle. Remove half the dough from the refrigerator. Roll it out to about 1/8-inch thickness. Cut out with cookie cutters. Repeat with the second half of the dough. Bake for about 8–10 minutes or until lightly brown around the edges.

For the glaze, mix the powdered sugar and water together. Add the food coloring if desired. Brush the glaze over the cookies while they're still warm.

CHRISTMAS IN ANY LANGUAGE

From Heartie Louise Tucker Jones

O ne of my favorite Christmas traditions is baking and sharing homemade goodies. One year, just before Christmas, a new family moved into our neighborhood. Since I was already baking some Christmas teacakes covered with red, green, and yellow sugar crystals, I made an extra dozen for our new neighbors. I placed them in a decorative jar and tied a festive red ribbon around the top.

Planning a trip to town, I decided to drop off the jar of colorful teacakes on my way. Since most of our neighbors were young couples with children, I was surprised when an elderly gentleman who was Chinese greeted me at the door in broken English. I tried to explain the reason for my gift—to welcome them to our neighborhood—but Mr. Chung's eyes filled with confusion. This wasn't the quick stop I had planned. I wanted to plunk the jar of sweets into my neighbor's hands, wish him a Merry Christmas, and be on my way, but communication proved difficult.

Outside of my native tongue, I was fairly fluent in Spanish, had survival skills in French and knew a few German phrases. I even remembered sparse greetings in Russian and Japanese, but I didn't know a single word of Chinese.

Mr. Chung followed me to the car, asking me to point out the exact house in which I lived. After several tries with words, pointing, and gestures, he seemed content in knowing who I was and where I lived. He returned to his house and I jumped into my car, anxious to get to my appointment.

The following Saturday, my doorbell rang and there stood Mr. Chung along with his petite wife and their adult daughter who spoke flawless English. "My parents wanted to thank you for your kindness," she said, as I opened the door and invited them inside. Mr. Chung presented me with a package of Santa cookies and Mrs. Chung gave a slight bow and offered a greeting in Chinese.

As we sat in the living room chatting, my oldest son came into the room carrying his little brother on his shoulders. Mrs. Chung's face suddenly lit up and her hands automatically extended toward Jay, my toddler. Then, seeming embarrassed to have displayed such emotion, she sat back against the sofa but continued to watch Jay for the rest of their visit.

In the months following Christmas, Mrs. Chung and I became friends. And though she never spoke a word of English, we were always welcomed into her home, especially Jay. She seemed to take great delight in his presence. Not being able to converse with Mrs. Chung, I never knew for certain what caused her sweet reaction to Jay on that Christmas visit in our home. But I have always believed that my little son with Down syndrome somehow reminded my new neighbor of her own children and grandchildren, and a homeland far away, on that most holy holiday.

7

TIME TO STIR UP YOUR FRIENDS

*C*hristmastime was always busy in Hope Valley, but this year was extra challenging for Jack Thornton. Beyond his Mountie duties, he'd also agreed to find permanent housing for all the new settlers. And he had promised to have everyone settled in time for Christmas. Bitter cold weather had added an extra urgency to his mission.

So he stirred up some friends and asked for help. Along with the other men from Hope Valley, he used every spare moment—patching holes, sawing wood, and supervising all the details needed to get the houses ready for their new occupants. But as anyone knows who has ever worked on an old house, there are surprises between every doorjamb to mess up your timeline.

What do you do when hidden challenges complicate your life? You do what Jack did—you link shoulders and hammers with like-hearted allies. Teamwork is the only way towns get built and mountains get scaled—and the beauty of this is that each of us has different God-given talents at our disposal. When we use those gifts for Him, something wonderful happens, because not only does the work get completed, but we end up encouraging each other as we labor together.

What is the town or mountain that you need to conquer? Pray and ask the Lord for help. And then put together a team that can do big things to change the world for good ... and for God.

And let us consider how to stir up
one another to love and good works,
not neglecting to meet together, as is the habit
of some, but encouraging one another.

HEBREWS 10:24–25 ESV

Dear Father, sometimes I get started on tasks for you and I try to do everything by myself. And then I get frustrated, weary, and discouraged. Remind me that you've given different gifts to everyone, and that when we join together and each of us uses our God-given talents, we can accomplish amazing things for you. Help me to be an encourager to others as we work together for you. Amen.

THE GIFT OF YOUR HEART

* Why does it make your tasks harder when you try to do them under your own strength?

* God's given different talents to each of us. How does that impact those of us who love Him?

RASPBERRY SALSA AND TORTILLA CHIPS

From the Kitchen of Heartie Lorraine Sherlin

A charming café in my hometown served raspberry salsa. I tried it and loved it. So I went home and experimented and came up with my own super simple version. I've served it many times at parties, church events, and weddings, and folks always love it. (Nobody has to know that it's this easy to prepare.)

INGREDIENTS

16 oz. raspberry jam (without seeds)
16 oz. bottle of chunky salsa
Tortilla chips

PREPARATION

Whisk together half the raspberry jam and the salsa. Continue adding raspberry jam until you reach your desired sweetness. Put into a pretty bowl and serve with tortilla chips.

Quick and Easy Entertaining Ideas

We've all experienced those moments when company unexpectedly arrives during the holidays. Here are a few ideas for snacks that you can serve in just a few minutes, so plan ahead and keep these items on hand for those unexpected visitors.

- *Line baskets with pretty holiday napkins and fill them with pretzels, popcorn, nuts, or chips.*
- *Buy cubed cheeses to keep on hand. Arrange them on a festive platter with a variety of crackers.*
- *Purchase biscuits or mini croissants. Slice them and add honey-glazed ham or smoked turkey.*
- *Spoon a jar of orange marmalade over a block of cream cheese. Serve with gingersnaps.*

Trash Bags Filled
with Kindness

From Heartie Amy Brown

We were raised to help those around us. We were taught that if someone was hungry, we should share our snack, and if someone was struggling, we should help them. Our parents lived by this code. My dad was forever helping people as he could, by welding, painting, doing excavation work, mowing fields, and so on.

We'd always had food, clothes, a warm home, and loving family, but when I was about fifteen or sixteen, we encountered some financial difficulties. It was okay, though. My younger sister and I knew this and were fine.

I'd always wake up early on Christmas morning to hang out with Dad, drinking good old-fashioned instant coffee. That morning, Dad went to let our dog out, and when he did, he noticed a bunch of filled trashed bags outside the door. There was a set of footprints coming up the driveway and heading back the other way.

Dad called for mom, and as we opened the bags, we realized they were filled with toys. It was so special yet mind-boggling as well. Dad put his boots on and went outside to investigate the footprints, but there was no evidence as to who had brought the bags. Just one trash bag per child with gifts inside.

We spread the gifts under the tree with tears in our eyes. My parents were baffled. Dad had suspicions about who had delivered the bags filled with love, kindness, and gifts, but nobody would claim responsibility.

My siblings awoke soon thereafter, and as we all attacked the pile of presents, paper began to fly. My sister and I got boom boxes with cassette tapes as well as cool sweatshirts. Our brothers got huge fire engines and other little toys. We never learned the identity of the kind soul who created such a magical Christmas for us, but that special person left such an impact on me—and to this day, I still practice random acts of kindness.

CARDINALS FOR CHRISTMAS

From Heartie Debbie Welch

*I*n 2002, two young friends of mine lost their grandmother. I attended her memorial service and learned how much she loved cardinals. After that whenever I saw a cardinal, I remembered the loss those girls must be feeling, so that Christmas, I decided to make happy memory triggers for them, using the red cardinal as a theme.

Each Christmas I began leaving notes and cardinal gifts on their doorstep from their Secret Santa and grandmother. Through the years those gifts included ornaments, figurines, plates, trinkets, notecards, or whatever touched my heart. When the youngest of the girls graduated from high school, my cardinal gift-giving finally came to an end. It had gone on for fourteen years.

I heard that years later, their mother hosted a holiday open house and the bounty of red birds on display was a sight to behold. When she explained how the collection was achieved, I hope hearts were warmed as they thought about a special grandmother who'd been remembered throughout the years.

8

GINGERBREAD AMENDS

*D*r. Carson Shepherd's Christmas efforts to break through to Myra McCormick's frosty heart took a while. But once the thaw started, an obvious change occurred, and the citizens of Hope Valley were probably stunned to see a smile on her face.

You can imagine Carson's surprise when he walked into the infirmary and discovered Myra sitting there across from a Yuletide supper she'd made for him. There was a new softness about her, a charm he'd not seen before. The meal was a way to make restitution for her gruff responses when he'd tried to help Myra past her bitterness at losing her husband.

But Myra had other amends she needed to offer—to the school children who'd tried to serenade her with Christmas carols. She had slammed the door in their surprised faces, and now she knew she needed to make it up to them. So she baked gingerbread cookies for the kids and handed them out at the Christmas parade, acknowledging how wrong she had been. When the children forgave her without hesitation, it melted her heart all over again.

God's heart is grieved when we hurt others. For them, but also for us because He knows how bitterness can take root and harden our souls. The truth is, hurt people … hurt people. And the holidays can be an especially painful time for fractured relationships. Making amends is the best medicine for the hurt we do to others—and even better medicine for our own wounded hearts.

Bear with each other and forgive one another
if any of you has a grievance against someone.
Forgive as the Lord forgave you. And over all
these virtues put on love, which binds them
all together in perfect unity.

COLOSSIANS 3:13-14 NIV

*Dear Lord, sometimes I do such foolish things and I end up
hurting those I love. When I mess up, help me to make
amends and seek the forgiveness of those I've wronged. Help
me to say those difficult words "I'm sorry!" with genuine
repentance. And let me also be quick to forgive others
whenever they cause me hurt. Amen.*

THE GIFT OF YOUR HEART

❊ **How does bitterness hurt you more than it
hurts the other person?**

❊ **How can forgiving others help to heal your
heart as well?**

From the Kitchen of Heartie Michelle Cox

INGREDIENTS

3 1/2 cups all-purpose flour
1 cup sugar
1 1/2 teaspoon baking powder
1 1/2 teaspoon salt
1 teaspoon cinnamon
1 teaspoon ginger

1 cup butter, softened
1/4 cup molasses
1 egg, lightly beaten
3 tablespoons orange juice
1 1/2 tablespoons milk
1 teaspoon vanilla

Frosting

2 tablespoons butter, softened
2 cups powdered sugar
1/2 teaspoon orange extract

3–4 tablespoons of orange
    juice
1 tablespoon fresh orange zest

PREPARATION

Preheat the oven to 350 degrees. Mix the flour, sugar, baking powder, salt, cinnamon, and ginger together in a large mixing bowl. Cut the butter into the flour mixture with a pastry blender (or two knives held side by side). Add the molasses, egg, orange juice, milk, and vanilla; mix well. I use a large wooden spoon to mix everything, and once the flour mixture has been incorporated with the liquid ingredients, I knead it in the bowl about 10–12 times until it's smooth and forms a ball.

Cut the dough in half, wrap, and place in the refrigerator to chill for an hour. Remove one half at a time and roll it out on a floured surface until it's about 1/8-inch thick. Cut with a gingerbread man cookie cutter and place on an ungreased cookie sheet. Bake at 350 degrees for 5–8 minutes or until lightly browned around the edges. Remove from the cookie sheet and place on a cooling rack.

While the cookies are cooling, make the frosting, mixing together the softened butter, powdered sugar, and the orange extract. Add the orange juice a little at a time until the desired consistency is reached, and then add the orange zest. Tint with food coloring if desired and decorate the cookies as you wish.

A DICKENS OF
A CHRISTMAS

From Heartie Brian Bird

I love reading Charles Dickens. His novels *David Copperfield* and *Great Expectations* were very influential in my formation as a young writer back in college. But it was *A Christmas Carol* that always left the deepest mark on me—and its influence has been felt on storytelling worldwide since it was first published in 1843.

Frank Capra's 1939 *It's a Wonderful Life*, everybody's favorite Christmas movie of all time, is an homage to the Dickens novella. And a little-known fact is that *A Christmas Carol* is the most presented stage play on the planet, even today. Community theaters all over the world perform *A Christmas Carol* as a way to raise the funds that keep them afloat the rest of the year.

So it was with deep reverence that I accepted an invitation in 2012 to witness a one-man performance of *A Christmas Carol* by none other than Gerald Charles Dickens—the great-great-grandson of Charles Dickens.

Gerald Charles Dickens is an actor from England, and each year he takes his family legacy on a tour across America because he is so devoted to the message of faith, hope, and love in *A Christmas Carol*.

When you witness his moving, emotional performance

of all the roles and voices in the play, you learn a great secret about Charles Dickens himself. Before the book was ever published, Charles Dickens believed in the message of redemption and generosity in his play so much that he would perform it himself—just as his great-great-grandson does today—traveling around England, becoming Ebenezer Scrooge, Bob Cratchit, Marley the Ghost, and Tiny Tim for audiences large and small. He would perform the scenes in private homes, cafés, hospitals, and orphanages—wherever anyone would pay attention.

Today, the traditions we love most—from Christmas trees, gift-giving, family gatherings, and bountiful meals—all owe their inspiration to *A Christmas Carol* and to Charles Dickens. What I love most about my experience shaking the hand of the great-great-grandson of one of my literary heroes is knowing I glimpsed the history of a storyteller considered by many to be "the man who invented Christmas."

9

LOVE WRAPPED
IN SWADDLING CLOTHES

Cody Stanton was thrilled with the gift Rosemary and Lee brought him from their honeymoon. His face said it all when they gave him a baseball signed by his favorite player, Doc Crandall. He treasured that baseball.

At school, the students chattered about what they wanted for Christmas. For instance, Maggie hoped for a Bitty Betsy doll like the one she'd lost moving to Hope Valley. Miss

Thatcher took the opportunity to announce Kindness Week as a way to teach the children that giving is better than receiving.

When an old peddler, Sam Bailey, came to town with his wagon full of "Notions & Wares," Cody spotted a Bitty Betsy doll on his wagon. He pulled out his money, hoping to buy it for Maggie, but when he realized the price was more than he had, he offered his beloved baseball as a trade for the doll.

Isn't that just exactly what God did for us at Christmas? He gave up His beloved Son because He loved us so much. To Him, *we* were worth the sacrifice. Think about that for a moment. You probably have many friends you love dearly—but would you give up one of your children for them? It would be such an unfair choice for any of us to have to make, and yet God made that choice for us. Unconditional love wrapped in swaddling clothes. Because He thought we were worth it. No other gift will ever rival that one.

For God so loved the world that he gave his
one and only Son, that whoever believes in him
shall not perish but have eternal life.

JOHN 3:16 NIV

*Dear Father, your love for us amazes me. I can't even
comprehend that kind of love—but I'm so grateful for it.
Help me to love like you do. Thank you for your gift to
the world … to me. I'm grateful there's enough love for
everyone. Help me to be faithful to tell others about
how much you love us. Amen.*

THE GIFT OF YOUR HEART

* God thought you were worth the sacrifice of His
  Son. How does that make you feel?

* How can you love like God does?

CHOCOLATE COCONUT PIE

From the Kitchen of Heartie Barb Waikel

Barb's family loves this pie, and she says it never stays around long.

INGREDIENTS

2 squares of semi-sweet chocolate
2 cups of whipped topping, thawed and divided
3/4 cup of flaked coconut, divided
1 graham cracker pie crust
1 box of coconut cream pudding (not instant)
1 1/2 cups cold milk
A few mini chocolate morsels

PREPARATION

Unwrap the chocolate squares and then microwave the chocolate in a medium-sized microwave-safe bowl for one minute, stirring every 30 seconds until the chocolate is melted. (Tip: The squares of chocolate are usually found in the baking section near the chocolate chips. Those who are more of the milk chocolate persuasion might want to use two squares of milk chocolate instead of the two squares of semi-sweet chocolate.) Add one cup of whipped topping and 1/4 cup of coconut. Stir until the mixture is blended well. (I fold it in rather than stirring it.) Spread the mixture onto the bottom of the graham cracker crust and set aside.

Add the pudding mix and the milk to a medium-sized saucepan until the mixture comes to a full boil; stir constantly so it doesn't scorch. You'll be able to tell when it starts thickening. Pour it gently over the chocolate mixture. Refrigerate for around four hours.

Top the pie with the remaining whipped topping and the 1/2 cup of coconut. Mini chocolate morsels can also be added as an extra topping. If you love chocolate and coconut, you'll love this pie.

A GIFT OF LOVE
FOR CHRISTMAS

From Heartie Melanie MacInnes
(The MacInnes family owns the farm
where *When Calls the Heart* is filmed.)

When I was growing up, my parents always hosted a Christmas Eve open house. The basement was where people would gather around the Christmas tree, and the children were allowed to choose one gift to open early.

One Christmas Eve when I was about six years old, I particularly remember the gift I chose to open that evening. I had been eyeing it all night. It was quite large, and I thought I'd seen my grandma—who I loved dearly—place it under the tree. When it came my turn to choose, I rushed straight to that gift. I saw the sparkle in Granny's eyes, and I remember her watching intently as I opened it.

So I carefully unwrapped the gift, as she always liked to keep any wrapping paper to reuse it for the following year. It was a box with rainbow wallpaper covering the outside and inside of the box. I soon realized the box was meant to be a crib. I started getting very excited, and as I looked into the box I was shocked to see what sort of looked like a Strawberry Shortcake doll. I was completely and utterly obsessed with Strawberry Shortcake when I was young.

But the doll I was looking at had greenish olive color skin, not light pink like on the show, and her hair was sewn on with an orangey, rusty color wool—not the striking signature red I was accustomed to. Her clothes were lovely, sewn carefully with Strawberry Shortcake's dress, but different. She had dangly arms and legs complete with hand-knitted green and white stockings. As I stared at this doll that I'd always wished for—but was not quite right—I burst into tears. I couldn't stop it, the tears just erupted out of me. She didn't look anything like the Strawberry Shortcake I knew from the cartoons I watched.

I turned my head and saw Granny. Her face looked so sad, and she explained to me that the material she used looked different under her light and the wool had appeared red. It wasn't her explanation that made me stop crying, but her face. It was the first time I remember feeling empathy and shame.

I started thinking about how hard she had worked on this doll. I could see it in her face. I looked more carefully at the doll, her little knitted green and white socks, the freckles on her face, the way her eyes appeared to shine.

I remember the moment so profoundly. After seeing Granny's sad face, I turned back to the doll and said, "I love her!" And I did—it was the love Granny had put into the doll that made me love her. I have very few toys from my childhood, but my green Strawberry Shortcake doll is still my favorite Christmas gift I've ever received.

10

A GIFT OF PURE LOVE

Cody had a problem. It was the first Christmas since Abigail Stanton had adopted him and Becky, and he wanted to do something special for his new mom—something worthy of their first Christmas as a family.

He didn't have money to buy anything nice, and even if he had, he couldn't think of what to get her. So he talked to Miss Thatcher. She reassured Cody that having him and his sister in her life was all the gift Abigail would ever need, but he still wanted a memorable present for her.

That's when he found Abigail's late son Peter's Christmas wish list in a box of mementos, and discovered the perfect gift for her—a trip to the North Pole that Peter dreamed about as a boy. That came as a North Pole float in the Hope Valley Christmas parade. Cody's face beamed when Abigail saw the gift of pure love he'd created for her.

Have you ever felt so much gratitude to God that you wanted to offer something back to Him? Similar to what Cody experienced, there really isn't anything big enough for that gift, is there? But here's the good news: God already has everything He needs. But the one thing He treasures above all is that you love Him, not out of obligation or guilt, but just because you do. That's the one gift that's guaranteed to touch His heart. He'll see it for what it is—a gift of pure love.

Love the Lord your God with all your heart
and with all your soul and with all your mind
and with all your strength.

MARK 12:30 NIV

Dear Lord, you've been so good to me, and I so want to do
something to show you how much I appreciate your blessings
and how much I love you. But no gift is good enough for
that. All I have to bring you is my heart. I'm willing for you
to use my life in whatever way you desire, even if it takes me
far out of my comfort zone. Amen.

THE GIFT OF YOUR HEART

* **There really isn't any gift big enough to express
  your gratitude to God. What can you give Him
  that will touch His heart?**

* **How can you take your love for Him and put it
  into action?**

CITRUS SPICED CASHEWS

From the Kitchen of Heartie Michelle Cox

Do you like to give homemade treats to your family and friends? Well, here's an original recipe that's sure to please and simple to prepare. My husband and I went to a large specialty grocery store awhile back. They sold warm citrus spiced cashews and they were absolutely delicious—and very expensive for a small quantity. I came home and experimented until my husband and I agreed I'd nailed the flavor with this recipe. I hope you enjoy them.

INGREDIENTS

1/4 cup water
1/2 teaspoon orange extract
1 cup granulated sugar
1/2 teaspoon apple pie spice
3 cups salted cashews

PREPARATION

Combine the water and orange extract in a large pan over medium heat. Add the sugar and apple pie spice; stir well. Add the cashews. (Tip: Purchasing a large jar of cashews at a big box discount store is usually much cheaper than buying the same quantity at the grocery store.) Stir until all the sugar is dissolved. Continue to cook and stir until the cashews are completely sugared with no syrup left in the pan. This usually takes about 13–15 minutes. Stir often. Don't try to turn the heat higher or they'll scorch. Spread on wax paper and let cool.

The Resurrected Spoon

From Carol Graham

*T*he year was 1987. My husband and I were going through a rough patch financially. Anything that could go wrong … did. No matter what we did to get ahead, we were thrown two steps back. We'd lost our business, and didn't have any income at the time. Every day seemed to bring a new dilemma.

It was Christmas, and there was hardly any money for gifts or a turkey dinner. Please don't misunderstand me. There are things a lot more important than exchanging gifts, but it was a harsh reminder of how difficult the year had been.

I tried not to show my concern, especially in front of the children, but then something happened. My favorite spoon that I used for cooking was a long-handled metal one with a rubber end to protect my hand from the heat. While preparing our dinner one evening, the rubber end broke off. Without warning, all the pent-up emotion of our circumstances poured out. I sat down on the floor and cried. When my husband heard me, he came into the kitchen and gently removed the broken spoon from my hand and then he took me in his arms and held me.

The next day was Christmas, and we woke up to a snowfall. We lived in a remote area surrounded by acres of woods. The beauty of the forest was breathtaking. What fun we had playing in the snow with our children! The freshness of the pure white snow seemed to send the message that this new year would be a new beginning. I found solace in that.

I hoped the children would understand why there were only some small gifts for them under the tree, and I certainly wished there could have been more—at least one of the bigger items they had put on their wish list. But I was thrilled knowing they had used their imagination to make a small token of love for each of us.

We finished opening the presents, and I went into the kitchen to prepare our dinner. Then I saw it. On the kitchen counter was my spoon—my favorite spoon. I couldn't believe my eyes. It had a new wooden handle. I had no idea where my husband got it or how he did it, but he had found a perfect piece of wood to fit the spoon. I got so excited that I believe the children were concerned that Mom had lost her marbles.

The lesson the children learned that day was priceless. They understood the joy that comes when giving a gift from the heart. That was over thirty years ago and I am still using that spoon. Every single day. We may never know the impact we have on someone's life from a small act of kindness. I know I will never forget what my husband's loving act that Christmas meant to me, because I'm reminded of it every time I use that spoon.

11

MUSIC TO GOD'S EARS

By Jordan Blackstone

*M*usic is an important part of Christmas. It began with the choir of angels who serenaded shepherds in a field on the night Jesus was born, and has continued through the millennia with beautiful carols and hymns. So when the town of Hope Valley decided to have a Christmas parade, they knew they had to have some music.

But when the volunteer band met at the saloon for their first practice, the result was anything but beautiful. Conductor Bill Avery did his best, but had serious doubts as to whether or not he could whip them into shape. Flutist Rosemary's entrance into the group made a big difference. Her on-key notes helped lead the others, and their practice and dedication led to a lovely result on the day of the parade.

Music always sets the tone for worship. This holiday season, stop and put on some faith-filled music as a way to make your celebration more meaningful. Listen to the lyrics about a silent night, about a town called Bethlehem, about a manger that served as a crib for the King of Kings.

But let's not stop there. Just as Rosemary inspired the other band members, we can inspire each other in our praise. There's something contagious about joining other people with voices uplifted in song—and there's nothing more beautiful than sitting in a room with Christmas lights glowing and the collective sound of a family's voices worshipping the One who is the reason for the season.

Praise the LORD. How good it is
to sing praises to our God,
how pleasant and fitting to praise him!
PSALM 147:1 NIV

Dear Lord, you are so worthy of our praise. Thank you for the amazing gift that you gave us on that Christmas so long ago. Put a song in our hearts that will overflow into the lives of others. Help me to listen to and embrace the words I'm singing as I worship you. And help that worship to be contagious in my daily life and in my home. Amen.

THE GIFT OF YOUR HEART

* **How can praise be contagious?**
* **How can faith-filled Christmas music lead your family to worship?**

CHICKEN SALAD IN PASTRY CUPS

From the Kitchen of Heartie Michelle Cox

INGREDIENTS

3 boxes mini "Fillo" shells (about 45 total)

2 cups stewed and diced chicken breasts

Approximately 1 1/2 cups mayonnaise

3/4 cup red seedless grapes, quartered

2 stalks celery, diced

Leaf lettuce or romaine

3/4 cup pecans, chopped

Salt, to taste

PREPARATION

Preheat the oven to 350 degrees. Place the mini "Fillo" shells on a cookie sheet. (Tip: The shells are found in the freezer section. Bake 3–5 minutes or until crisp. Set aside to cool.

Stew the chicken until it's tender and done; drain and let cool. Dice in small chunks, put in a mixing bowl and add about 1/2 cup of the mayonnaise to keep it from drying out. Refrigerate while you get the other ingredients ready.

Wash the grapes, celery and lettuce. Put them on paper towels to dry and then cut the grapes into quarters; set aside. Dice the celery into small pieces. And then tear the lettuce into small pieces that will fit inside the "Fillo" cups; set aside.

Add the grapes, pecans, and celery to the chicken and then keep adding mayonnaise until the mixture is creamy. Salt to taste; chill.

A few hours before serving, place a lettuce leaf in each "Fillo" shell and then add a teaspoon of the chicken salad. Put them on a pretty tray and enjoy.

PUTTING THE MERRY BACK IN CHRISTMAS

From Heartie Pam Farrel

*B*ill and I married on December 14. After our honeymoon, we carefully made our way down a snowy grade to the Reno airport. We were college kids with part-time jobs and big hopes—but no money. After our honeymoon, we were down to our last five dollars. We knew our family would pick us up and feed us, so even with just five dollars and no credit cards, we had a "God will provide" attitude.

We were a little concerned when we learned the blizzard had delayed flights for at least four hours. By this point, we were hungry. We only had that five dollars, but we knew they had a ninety-nine cent buffet. We ate as much as we could, not knowing when or where our next meal would come from. After paying the bill and tip, we had just two dollars.

Hour after hour passed with delay after delay. Cheerful Christmas holiday tunes blasted through the airport but the crowds of tired, worried passengers were anything but happy. Well, except for lovey-dovey us, and an elderly woman sitting near us crocheting.

We struck up a conversation, and the wisdom of her years was reflected in her attitude about the situation: "No need to worry or complain about things you have no control over."

We asked what she was crocheting and she replied, "Christmas wreaths to put on my family's tree for my grandkids."

"You seem to be the only happy woman in the airport. Bill and I feel for these bored little kids and their tired parents."

My husband said, "We work with youth. Let's see if they want to go caroling with us in the terminal."

Our newly-adopted grandmother said, "Then you'll need candy!" She took boxes of candy canes from her yarn bag and handed us at least twenty of the crocheted wreaths, showing us how to weave the candy cane into the ornament. "Give these to the kids who come caroling with you." And so we did. We went through the airport singing Christmas carols and gathering children—and many parents—to accompany us on our mission to put the merry back into Christmas.

Our growing band of ticketed passengers caroled from gate to gate to gate for about an hour, and smiles began to appear on faces. And while we belted a rousing chorus of "We Wish You a Merry Christmas," the announcement was made that all flights would be taking off. The crowds continued to sing as they made their way to their respective gates. Even as we boarded, we could hear "Joy to the World" echoing through the jet bridge.

The grandmother gave five round wreaths to us on the plane. "These are for you and the kids you'll have one day." And each Christmas, Bill and I would retell the story, and our three sons would hang their wreaths as we once again were reminded that joy is always a choice of the heart.

12

A CRIB FIT FOR A KING

*R*obert had one thought on his mind as he placed his ornament on the Christmas Wishing Tree. He wanted a crib
for the new baby arriving soon in his family. He was thrilled
when Miss Thatcher selected his ornament and Mountie Jack
pitched in to help him build a crib for his new baby brother
or sister.

Robert wasn't the only one looking for a special way to
welcome a new baby. Two millennia ago, Mary and Joseph
must have planned ahead for the child who would soon join

their family. Mary probably made little clothes and blankets for the child she'd soon hold in her arms. As a carpenter, Joseph likely crafted and polished a crib for his new son.

But God had other ideas in mind for Jesus' arrival. Instead of a warm, safe birth at home, Joseph and Mary were forced on a dusty road trip as birth pangs began to wrack her body. Instead of a beautifully-crafted crib, their new son would be placed into a lowly stable manger—a humble beginning and beautiful reminder that God's love is available to all, no matter our circumstances.

The question for us is "How do *we* welcome Him?" Is He our focus each day, or is He an afterthought? Just as Robert prepared that crib to welcome his new sibling, we should prepare our souls, sanding away imperfections and polishing our hearts, so that the Savior is always welcome in our lives.

Now when Jesus returned,
the crowd welcomed him,
for they were all waiting for him.

LUKE 8:40 ESV

Dear God, I so often get busy, and when I do, you sometimes get shoved to the margins of my life. I find myself not praying and not reading your Word as much as I should. I don't plan it that way, but sometimes circumstances just get in the way. Please help me to keep you at the forefront of my life. I want the welcome mat to always be out for you and I want to be waiting for you always. Amen.

THE GIFT OF YOUR HEART

∗ **Why do you think God arranged it for His Son to be born in a lowly stable?**

∗ **What steps can you take to welcome God into your day?**

CANDY CANE COOKIES

From the Kitchen of Heartie Kami Clements

INGREDIENTS

- 1/2 cup soft shortening
- 1/2 cup soft butter (or you can use 1 cup all butter instead of using the shortening)
- 1 cup sifted powdered sugar
- 1 egg
- 1 1/2 teaspoon almond flavoring
- 1 teaspoon vanilla
- 2 1/2 cups all-purpose flour
- 1/2 teaspoon salt
- 1/2 teaspoon red food coloring
- About 1/2 cup sugar
- 1/2 cup crushed peppermints

PREPARATION

Mix the shortening and the softened butter, the powdered sugar, egg, almond flavoring, and vanilla until well blended. Sift the flour and the salt together and add it to the butter mixture. Divide the dough in half and place it in separate bowls. Add the red food coloring into the dough in one bowl. Mix until it's well blended. Chill for about an hour (but no longer than that).

Roll about one teaspoon of each color into strips about four inches long. Press the ends lightly together, twist the pieces like a rope, and create a crook. Place the cookies on an ungreased cookie sheet. Bake them at 375 degrees for about nine minutes or until they are lightly browned.

While the cookies bake, stir the sugar and crushed peppermints together; set aside. When the cookies are done, remove them to a cooling rack, and while they're still warm, sprinkle with the mixture of sugar and peppermint.

THE WORLD'S MOST
SPECIAL BARBIE DOLLS

From Heartie Marnie Swedberg

When my mom and dad were the young, penniless parents of four little girls, they came across an entire box of naked Barbie dolls at a rummage sale. After first looking away, my mother had an idea, bought the dolls, and started sewing during every spare minute, using every scrap of fabric she could find.

Christmas that year was our most memorable, as four wide-eyed daughters came down the stairs into a living room full of Barbie dolls dressed in the most amazing gowns, outfits, pajamas, and more. They were everywhere! As adults, we still marvel at our mother's ingenuity and tireless creativity to accomplish such a special Christmas surprise for all of us.

MY FAVORITE CHRISTMAS TRADITION

From Heartie Deb DeArmond

*E*very year on Christmas Eve, we each open one package. The oldest children play "Santa" and distribute them, one at a time. As each person receives his or her gift, the remaining family members tell them how they've been "a gift" to them.

Sometimes my boys have recalled something from the way-back machine. Something like, "You introduced me to your friends when I was scared my first few days of junior high and I never forgot it. And you checked in with me to make sure I was finding my way and invited me to sit with your friends at lunch. I don't know that I ever thanked you."

Or sometimes it's very current, "I appreciated the love you showed me this year after the miscarriage. You kept me company for the first couple of days, just being present. You watched old movies with me and let me know I wasn't alone. I don't know that I could have gotten through that without you."

And sometimes it's not so much about "what you did" but more about "who you are." For example, "I've always been proud to call you my dad. You helped so many of my friends who didn't have a father in their life."

Those words are true gifts from the heart, and we're never done till we've shed a few tears along the way. It's one of my favorite things each Christmas.

13

WHEN DREAMS
THE HEART

Children have no trouble coming up with wish lists for Christmas. Even as adults we still often make lists of things we want, or need. But in Hope Valley that Christmas, there was just one thing on Elizabeth's list: She wanted Jack home for the holidays. She fretted and prayed about it, but didn't really expect to have her wish fulfilled. She didn't think it could happen.

But then, while standing in front of the Christmas tree in town, it *did* happen. She turned around, and there he was. Her handsome Mountie was home, safe. Back from the war. She couldn't believe it.

The same is true of us spiritually. Sometimes we wish for things that seem impossible. Hopes and dreams that we really want to accomplish, but there are so many obstacles in the way that it looks hopeless. We fret. We pray. And sometimes we don't expect to have our prayers answered. But God operates in a much different way. He doesn't grant us everything we want. He loves us too much to do that. But He always gives us exactly what we need.

And just as Elizabeth's friends in Hope Valley took great delight in helping make Elizabeth's wish come true, God takes great delight in fulfilling the dreams and desires of our hearts—especially when our expectations are pure. So keep working. Keep hoping. Keep praying. Because one day you might just turn around and discover that God has made your impossible dream come true.

Blessed is the man who trusts in the LORD,
and whose hope is the LORD.

JEREMIAH 17:7 NKJV

Dear Father, I've discovered I'm not good at waiting. I've dreamed big things I'd like to accomplish, but time marches by without them always coming to fruition—and yet I feel like those dreams came from you. Give me hope in the waiting. Give me patience. Help me not to quit, but to wait on you, knowing that your timing is always best. Amen.

THE GIFT OF YOUR HEART

* Why are you sometimes surprised when God answers your prayers?

* Why does God delight in making your hopes and dreams become a reality?

AUSTRIAN LINZER COOKIES

From the Kitchen of Heartie Leslie Turner

INGREDIENTS

- 1 cup butter, softened
- 1 cup sugar
- 2 egg yolks
- 1 cup ground pecans
- 1 lemon rind, finely grated
- 2 cups all-purpose flour
- 1 teaspoon cinnamon
- 1/2 teaspoon ground cloves
- Jam, various flavors

PREPARATION

Cream the softened butter and the sugar until the mixture is light and fluffy. Add the two egg yolks; blend until incorporated. Stir in the ground pecans and the grated lemon rind. Grate the lemon rind right before using so it doesn't turn brown.

Sift all of the dry ingredients together and then add them to the butter mixture; blend well. Chill the dough for about 30 minutes, and then drop in teaspoon-sized amounts onto an ungreased cookie sheet. Make a small indentation in the top of each cookie with your thumb or with the back of a spoon and put about a half teaspoon of jam on top of each cookie. (I used seedless raspberry jam for this and it was awesome.) Bake at 350 degrees for 10–15 minutes or until lightly browned.

THE CHRISTMAS STORM

From Heartie Shirley Ann Hurley

*I*n our little town of Bonney Lake, Washington, we were about ready for our evening outdoor program of the Christmas story, complete with live animals, singing, full costumes which I had personally made, and lighting. The opening was always so beautiful with the sounds of Trans-Siberian Orchestra's "Christmas Canon." Everything was going to be perfect except for the worry of the high winds that were all around us, so we did the only thing we knew to do—we prayed.

One hour before we were to start, we were at the church getting ready, and then the storm hit, with huge winds that ripped our stable right out of the ground and tossed it over the fence into the neighbor's yard. The sky turned dark and ugly and the winds grew stronger.

Everyone looked at me, wondering what to do. Should we cancel? I looked in disbelief at what was happening around me. The animals started to arrive, and I was still questioning what we should do. There was a covered area in front of the doors of our church. We could move there. We had a back-drop we could use, and maybe it would work.

As I looked out at the storm, I noticed many of our church members showing up to help. They retrieved the blown-away stable. We moved our enclosed fences for the animals, put up our backdrop, and set up our sound and lighting. I changed where everyone would enter from, and then we were ready to go, just minutes from our start time.

And then our miracle happened. People actually came out in the storm for our outdoor nativity, and when we were ready to start and the beautiful "Christmas Canon" music started to play, the wind stopped. We got through the entire nativity with only a few little hiccups from our donkey.

We took photos for people, had hot chocolate and cookies, visited with everyone—and then, when we got everything safely inside, the wind started back up. I'm convinced that God performed a miracle for us that evening and calmed a storm in our little town of Bonney Lake while it blew everywhere else around us, so that we could stage our beautiful tribute to the birth of our heavenly King.

14

A CHRISTMAS DO-OVER

*H*enry Gowen could easily be called the black sheep of Hope Valley—a title he'd likely wear with pride. He seemed to thrive on being obnoxious and antagonistic, and he'd hurt many citizens over the years—from his negligence in the mine explosion, to his underhanded actions as mayor.

He knew the townspeople looked at him with fear and loathing, but that had always been okay with him. That is, until he encountered Abigail Stanton. He'd never met anyone like her. She was warm and loving, but had a backbone of steel as she fought for what was just and important. And she always looked for the good in others. Yes, even in Henry Gowen.

That touched something deep inside his hardened soul. Her kindness began to thaw his frozen heart. And then the unthinkable happened. He did a good deed—he fetched Abigail's daughter, Becky, stranded in a storm, and brought her home for Christmas—something nobody in Hope Valley ever expected.

Perhaps you have a past like Henry. Maybe you feel that you have too many marks against you, and there's no hope for you. The truth is, it's never too late for redemption. God doesn't expect perfection. He knows how hard it is to get it all right in this world. That's exactly why that baby in the manger came—He makes everything right if we will just offer our past to Him, and ask for a Henry Gowen do-over.

I will give them a heart to know me, that I am the
Lord. They will be my people, and I will be their
God, for they will return to me with all their heart.

JEREMIAH 24:7 NIV

*Dear God, I mess up so often. I'm sure I've grieved you so
many times. If I'm honest, I must admit that there have been
occasions when I've been upset with you, instances when I've
wandered away from you. There have even been times when
I've wondered if you could forgive me for the wrongs that I've
done—but I'm so grateful for the assurance that your mercies
are new every morning, and for the peace that brings. Amen.*

THE GIFT OF YOUR HEART

* Why did Abigail's kindness touch Henry's
  heart—and what can you learn from that?

* How does God respond when you come to Him
  with a heart of repentance?

WHITE CHOCOLATE COFFEE

From the Kitchen of Heartie Michelle Cox

My daughters-in-law were at the house one night, and we were looking through some magazines together. One of them said, "Wow, this white chocolate coffee sounds good! Let's make some." She read off the ingredients, but I was missing more than half of them. We decided to make up our own recipe using items I had in the pantry and refrigerator, and the result is this white chocolate coffee that's now a family must-have on Christmas Eve and cold winter days.

INGREDIENTS

1/2 cup whipping cream
2 cups milk
1/3 cup sugar
4 oz. white baking chocolate, finely chopped
2 1/2 cups freshly brewed coffee
Whipped cream
White chocolate curls or chocolate shavings

PREPARATION

Place the whipping cream, milk, sugar, and white chocolate in a saucepan. Simmer the mixture over medium heat until it begins to steam, but do not bring it to a boil. Add the coffee; stir. Top each cup with whipped cream and garnish with white chocolate curls or chocolate shavings. (Tip: This is best made fresh. You can stir the ingredients together ahead of time but wait until serving time to steam it. We've enjoyed experimenting by adding different types of chocolates or peppermint chips to the coffee. Use your imagination and see what flavors you can come up with!)

An Unexpected Christmas Hero

From Heartie Kathi Macias

*I*t was early 2012 when I first felt the stirrings to write a novel dealing with the topic of homelessness. Because I was known for my annual Christmas novels, I decided to make it my holiday offering for that year.

And so I began to research the topic, stunned by what I learned. Contrary to what many believe about the homeless population here in America, it isn't made up exclusively of lazy people who don't want to work. Most, in fact, would like to have a job and find their way out of living on the streets. And sadly, many of the homeless are families, including young children. That realization broke my heart and convinced me my book would be about a young family trying to stay safe and fed—and together.

It also occurred to me that I needed some sort of Christmas hero to help this little family find a permanent roof over their heads, and I immediately thought of the veterans, people who had sacrificed so much to fight for our country and defend our liberties, who now had nowhere to call home. With that in mind, I had my characters for the story.

Unexpected Christmas Hero came together quickly and was soon turned in to my publisher for production. When that process reached the point of cover design, the publisher sent their photographer and his wife out to search for someone who would resemble the story's hero. They walked the streets of the city where they lived, bundled up against the falling snow, praying God would send the right person.

Then they spotted him, a grisly, slightly beyond middle-aged man with graying hair and a beard. He wore a green Army jacket as he walked against the wind. When the photographer and his wife approached him, told him about the book, and asked if he'd help, he began to cry.

"Of course I will," he choked out. "I really am homeless, and I haven't seen my family in years. Maybe this will somehow help me find them."

It wasn't long before the man's picture graced the cover of *Unexpected Christmas Hero*, and I found out how he ended up there. *We have to find his family*, I thought, and so I mounted a social-network campaign to do just that. Sure enough, within a matter of weeks, I heard from one of his grown daughters, who wanted desperately to see him. We were able to get this dear man home to his family in time for Christmas, to see his two daughters again, and to meet his grandchildren for the first time.

As I rejoiced over the emailed pictures of our "unexpected hero" and his family, celebrating Christmas together, I worshipped with a renewed sense of gratitude and awe. We truly serve an amazing God, whose thoughts are so far above our own, whose plans for us are always good—and who loves to give us good gifts all year long.

PRAY FOR A MIRACLE ...
THEN BE THE MIRACLE

*C*hristmas had almost arrived, but that didn't mean anything to Nancy Tucker. She was in a dark place. Her
husband had died recently trying to save the settlement from
a horrible flood and mudslide. Of course, she missed the
feel of his hand in hers, and the sound of his voice and his
strength. But even more so, she knew the void it would leave in
their son Harper's heart. Life was just too hard and she didn't

see how she was going to make it through each day, let alone this season that was supposed to be joyous. Engrossed in her grief, she pushed everyone away.

Pastor Frank had been there when her husband took his last breath. But no matter how much he wanted to fix things for Nancy, he couldn't. She ran away, leaving the town behind—but not her sorrow. Elizabeth wondered what they could do to help, but then Jack had the answer, "We can pray for a miracle."

Those are difficult times when we love folks whose hearts are heavy and we don't know how to help. But we can tell them about our faithful God. And then we can pray for a miracle—because God is still in the miracle-working business today. But don't stop there. Maybe the miracle is actually *you*. God can use you as His hands and feet in the life of your friend or loved one this Christmas.

But Jesus looked at them and said,
"With man this is impossible,
but with God all things are possible."
MATTHEW 19:26 ESV

*Dear Lord, it hurts me when those I love are hurting.
I feel so helpless. Help me to worry less and pray more.
Give me the faith to pray for miracles and, if warranted,
to allow you to use me as part of the miracle you are
providing. Help me to quit looking at situations through
the lens of my limited capabilities, but instead, to see
that you are a God of limitless abilities. Amen.*

THE GIFT OF YOUR HEART

* **Why do you think you so often forget to pray for miracles?**

* **In what ways can God use you to be His hands and feet in the lives of others?**

MAMA'S FRUIT SALAD

From the Kitchen of Heartie Beverly Parrish

This makes a beautiful large bowl of fruit salad with a light syrupy sauce. It's very forgiving as far as amounts go, so you can add more of your favorite fruits and less of others. And feel free to add blueberries, raspberries, and peaches as desired.

INGREDIENTS

- 2 large cans of fruit cocktail in heavy syrup (don't drain!)
- 1 lb. (or more) of seedless grapes, halved (I buy both red and green for the extra color)
- 2 oranges, cut into segments
- 1 lb. of strawberries, sliced
- 2 apples, peeled and diced
- 3 bananas, peeled and sliced
- 1/2 cup sugar (more if desired)

PREPARATION

Combine the fruit cocktail (with the juice from the cans), the halved grapes, orange segments, strawberries, apples, and bananas. (Tip: After cutting the oranges into segments, squeeze the juice from the leftover orange pieces and add the juice to the bowl of fruit salad.) Start with adding half a cup of sugar, and then keep adding sugar until your desired taste is reached. It's hard to give an exact amount for the sugar since fruit is sometimes sweeter than others.

LIGHTS FOR CHRISTMAS

From Heartie Michelle Cox

*T*he snow began falling on December 17. It was beautiful as it covered everything in a blanket of pristine white. The trees in the woods around our house looked as if God had sprinkled powdered sugar on them.

Yes, it was gorgeous, but the flakes continued to fall … and fall … and fall. The wet snow began to weigh down the branches of the trees, and soon loud cracks were heard as limbs started snapping.

We'd been through this before, so we knew there was a good chance that we'd be without power before too long. We quickly began our snowstorm prep, gathering lanterns and candles, and carrying firewood in so it would be dry. Sure enough, just as we finished our preparations, the power clicked off, and the cheery lights on our Christmas tree went dark.

The first day without power wasn't too bad. Even the second day wasn't too uncomfortable or dreary, but as day after day without power went by, our spirits began to droop. By this time, the food in the refrigerator and freezer had thawed and spoiled, and food choices were becoming more and more limited.

All of us were a bit aggravated. We had places to go and things to do. After seven days without power, I called our electric company on the morning of Christmas Eve to see if they had any idea when everything would be back to normal. The news from the other end of the phone was not what I wanted to hear as the employee said it would likely be at least three more days. Three days? That meant we'd have to cancel our Christmas plans. There'd be no opening gifts by the light of the Christmas tree and no big family holiday meal.

I was devastated. This was our first grandchild's first Christmas. I'd had such big plans for our family. When a friend from my speaker's group called to check on us, I asked her to send a message to our prayer loop to pray that the lights would come back on soon. She said she'd do that right away. I started getting phone calls from those dear ladies, telling me they were praying.

Forty-five minutes after that prayer request went out, I heard something unusual. I opened the front door so I could listen, and then I realized it was the sound of big truck engines. Moments later, a stream of trucks from our electric company drove through the neighborhood, and an hour later, we had power again.

We had just enough time to get to the grocery store before it closed, and we returned home with a ham and everything else we needed for our big family Christmas dinner.

And that night, as our loved ones gathered and we enjoyed our beautifully-lit tree in a warm house, I looked around the room with tears in my eyes—grateful beyond words for the Christmas when prayer turned the lights back on.

16

NEVER BE AFRAID
TO GO HOME

By Jordan Blackstone

When Jack arrived home in Hope Valley from the Northwest Territories for a few days of "R & R" at Christmas, it was the little things he appreciated, and had missed most.

He revealed something to Elizabeth that he'd discovered while gone: "Being away from home makes you grateful for the things you left behind." He'd experienced the loneliness of being away from those he loved. He'd missed his new fiancée, seeing her sweet face across the table as they shared shepherd's pie, and hearing her laughter.

And he'd missed the townsfolk: chuckling with Lee over Rosemary's latest escapade; the cooking at Abigail's café; the school children at play; and the Mountie salutes he would always get from Cody and Robert.

They were all things easily taken for granted before his deployment north, but not anymore. Now he saw those everyday moments as priceless gifts from God.

Sometimes it takes being away to realize how precious home is. But here's a secret: you don't have to leave home to grasp that. Take a step back and really see how God has blessed you. Look at the family He's given you (as imperfect as they are), the friends who add so much to your life, and the love and laughter that fills your days.

Soak up the everyday blessings of home. In the midst of your busy Christmas, make sure you don't miss those precious, irreplaceable moments that God has given to you.

Now therefore may it please you to bless
the house of your servant, so that it may continue
forever before you. For you, O Lord God,
have spoken, and with your blessing shall
the house of your servant be blessed forever.

2 Samuel 7:29 esv

*Dear Father, sometimes I don't stop to consider how
abundantly you've blessed me. Thank you for my home.
For people who love me. For friends who bless me and fill my
life in so many ways. For the family that gives me so much
joy. Help me to never take my home and family for granted.
And thank you for the special time of Christmas. For the
priceless gift of your Son. And for the wonderful memories
we make as we celebrate His birth. Amen.*

The Gift of Your Heart

❋ **Why do you sometimes fail to see the everyday
blessings God's given to you?**

❋ **Why do you think God chooses to bless you so
abundantly?**

SHEPHERD'S PIE

From the Kitchen of Heartie Vikki Banks

This recipe will fill a 13x9x2 casserole dish. For a smaller family, cut the recipe in half and it will fit well in a pie pan. (Note from Michelle: When I tested this, I added 1/4 tsp. of paprika that wasn't in Vikki's recipe, but we couldn't upset Miss Thatcher, now could we? And, no, there isn't any lard in there.)

INGREDIENTS

2 lbs. ground beef
1 tablespoon olive oil
1 1/2 cups chopped sweet onion
3/4 cup chopped green pepper
1 teaspoon minced garlic
1 cup ketchup
2 tablespoons Worcestershire sauce

1/4 teaspoon paprika
1 tablespoon thyme
1 tablespoon oregano
Salt and pepper, to taste
16 oz. bag of frozen mixed vegetables
1 1/2 cups beef broth/stock
2 pouches dry brown gravy mix

Mashed Potato Topping

4 cups boiling water
4 oz. package of roasted garlic instant potatoes
4 oz. package of baby reds instant potatoes
1 stick of butter
Sour cream, if desired
2 cups shredded cheddar cheese
2–3 tablespoons milk, optional

PREPARATION

Preheat the oven to 350 degrees. In a large nonstick skillet over medium-high heat, add the olive oil and the ground beef. Stir in the chopped onion, green peppers, and the minced garlic. Cook until browned and thoroughly done. Drain well and remove any excess fat by patting the ground beef with a paper towel. Add the ketchup,

Worcestershire sauce, paprika, thyme, and oregano. Mix well and then add the frozen vegetables.

Combine the beef broth and brown gravy mix in a cup and pour over the ground beef and vegetable mixture. Cover and simmer on medium to medium-low for approximately 20 minutes, stirring occasionally. Place in a 13x9x2 baking dish that has been coated with cooking spray.

Bring four cups of water to a boil. Add the two packages of instant potatoes; stir until mixed together. Add the stick of butter and stir until melted and combined. If the potatoes seem a little dry, add a couple of tablespoons of milk until they're smooth and creamy. Cover the ground beef mixture, swirling as if it were cake icing. Bake for 40–45 minutes at 350 degrees. Remove from the oven and sprinkle the cheddar cheese on top of the potatoes. Place back into the oven for a few minutes until the cheese is melted.

A Memorable
Christmas across
the Pond

From Heartie Karen Nennig

*I*n 1979, my husband, who served in the Air Force, received new orders for a small base in England. We'd only been married one year and hadn't accumulated much in the way of household goods, but what we did have was going to be packed up in September. We were told it would get to us by Halloween. So the waiting game began when we arrived in England. While we waited, we borrowed some furniture and basic items (dishes, pots and pans, etc.) from the base.

However, Halloween came and went … and no household goods. Then we were told they'd be there by Thanksgiving—but that also passed by and nothing arrived. I was discouraged.

We later learned we wouldn't even have our stuff in time for Christmas, so we had to figure out what to do for a tree. We had bought our artificial tree the year before and loved it, but the tree and all of our decorations were on a ship somewhere in the Atlantic Ocean.

We couldn't afford a real tree, so we borrowed a strand of Christmas beads from friends we'd recently met. We hung the beads on one of the living room walls in the shape of a Christmas tree, maybe about three feet tall. Then I cut Christmas wrapping paper into different shaped ornaments. I hung those ornaments on the tree with tape. Then I placed our borrowed coffee table against the wall where the tree was and covered the table with a borrowed white tablecloth. That way, we could put our presents to each other under the "tree."

It was the skimpiest tree and quite possibly the skimpiest Christmas I've ever had in my life, but I look back on that Christmas with such great happiness, knowing that we made it special and memorable because of the things we *did* ... and not because of the things we *had*.

A FAITHFUL REMINDER ON MY DOORSTEP

From Heartie Cheri Smith

Christmas has always been one of my favorite holidays. Who doesn't love singing Christmas carols, snuggling up in front of a fire, spending time with loved ones, and celebrating our Savior's birth?

And Christmas has taken on an even more special meaning since I walked through cancer six years ago in the fall of 2012. At the time, I wasn't sure what the outcome would be. I was believing for a miracle and trying to be strong for my family. And then, an anonymous gift was left on my doorstep—a beautiful blue and red ornament with the word "Faith" written on it, along with a card with a significant amount of money inside.

To this day, I don't know who left it there, but it blessed my family financially from the burden of my medical bills. It also gave us hope and reminded us to have faith that I would be healed. Every year since, I have put that ornament at the top of my tree to continually remind us that God is faithful in every situation.

17

WHEN THINGS FALL
APART AT CHRISTMAS

*E*lizabeth Thatcher was excited when she walked into Yost's
Mercantile carrying a long shopping list for the holidays.
She loved Christmas, and she loved her Hope Valley friends
and students. Elizabeth took great joy in planning Christmas
for all of them, especially the families living in a makeshift
settlement. They'd lost so much and were facing a less-than-
joy-filled Yuletide.

She couldn't wait to surprise them with gifts that would
fill their hearts. Her excitement built as Christmas neared ...
until she received some devastating news. The train would be

delayed! None of the gifts she'd chosen so carefully for her beloved students would be there. How would she explain it to them?

Just like Elizabeth, sometimes our hopes and dreams can crash at a moment's notice—and that can be painful at Christmas. Especially when it's a situation that we can't fix. That's when it's so important to remember that God's most important gift for us can never be taken from us: the gift of God's Son. It's the cure for everything that ails us.

God is never challenged by our circumstances and He will be "enough" for whatever we face. And because we have that hope, we can go to Him in prayer about everything, at Christmas, or any other day of the year, knowing that *nothing* is impossible for Him. *Immanuel* is the Hebrew word for "Messiah," but it also means "God with us." And He is ... forever and always.

For to us a child is born, to us a son is given,
and the government will be on his shoulders.
And he will be called Wonderful Counselor, Mighty
God, Everlasting Father, Prince of Peace.

ISAIAH 9:6 NIV

*Father, I want things to be wonderful for my loved ones—
especially at Christmas. It's heartbreaking when the funds
aren't there for gifts or when relationships are fractured.
Remind me that you are good ... even in the hard times.
Provide what I need, and help me to remember in my
sometimes impossible world, that you are a God
of all things possible. Amen.*

THE GIFT OF YOUR HEART

❋ Why do you sometimes focus more on your
problems than on the One who is your problem solver?

❋ How does it affect you to know that nothing is
impossible with God?

MOM'S RUSSIAN TEA

From the Kitchen of Vicky Gerald

My family has made this delicious Russian tea for more than sixty years now. This tastes so good on a cold winter day.

INGREDIENTS

9 cups water, divided
2 cinnamon sticks
2 teaspoons whole cloves
10 small tea bags
2 cups sugar
1 large can of pineapple juice
24 oz. of orange juice
1/2 cup of lemon juice

PREPARATION

In a small saucepan, add one cup of the water, the cinnamon sticks, and the whole cloves. Bring this to a boil and then reduce the heat and simmer for thirty minutes.

While that is simmering, put eight cups of water in a large pan and bring it to a boil. Remove the pot from the burner and add the ten tea bags. Let them steep and then remove the tea bags. Add the sugar; stir well and then add the pineapple juice, orange juice, and the lemon juice.

Remove the whole cloves from the simmered cup of water and pour the liquid into the tea mixture. Stir well and simmer until nice and hot.

Today's Mess-Ups Are Tomorrow's Memories

From Heartie Michelle Cox

Christmas is a special time, but sometimes things don't go quite as planned. I remember one year when I was out Christmas shopping with my husband. We received a phone call from our sons, and we could tell from their voices that something had happened.

It seems they'd been carrying the decorations down from our upstairs storage closet. As they unpacked the full-size red ceramic boots that my cousin had painted for me one year, they discovered that a flying squirrel had taken up residence there. Yeah, that caused a bit of excitement.

Then there was the year I opened my presents and I discovered some lovely burgundy pajamas from my husband. A few moments later when I opened the gift from our toddler son, I discovered that when Paul had taken Jason shopping, he'd bought the exact same pair of burgundy pajamas.

On another year, our Christmas was way different than normal. My husband had become deathly ill, spending a week in the hospital before having surgery, and then when he got home, he faced weeks of recuperation. With Christmas just weeks away, I knew I needed to start decorating the house so our sons wouldn't be disappointed.

Our oldest son was about sixteen at the time. I told Jeremy, "Dad can't do it this year, and I need to stay here with him, so you'll be in charge of going to the tree farm to find the perfect Christmas tree for us. I gave him the "make sure the tree is fresh and that the needles aren't falling off" speech, and then I reminded him to make sure that the tree was good and full.

That evening when he and his brother carried the trussed-up tree into our family room, the wonderful aroma of a freshly-cut Frasier fir filled the room. Propped up on pillows on the couch, Paul gave the boys directions as they fastened the tree into the stand. When they stood it up, it was too tall, so they had to get a saw and lop some off the bottom.

And then came the moment of truth as Jeremy began to cut the ropes that had tied the limbs in place—a moment that still makes me giggle twenty-five years later. Not only had he gotten a full tree, but when the ropes released the branches, they touched the walls on both sides and the tree took up over a third of the room. It was that big.

We laughed until our stomachs hurt that night. Normally, our tree limbs are crowded with ornaments, but the monster-sized tree was so big that when we decorated it, the branches looked bare.

Who would have thought that our most stressful Christmas season ever would become one of our best? But we made an important discovery from all the times when we had Christmas mayhem and mishaps—because we found that today's messed-up moments quite often become tomorrow's favorite memories.

CG 18 GD

CHOOSE HOPE,
PLAN ACCORDINGLY

A cloud hung over Jack and Elizabeth's Christmas Eve
supper table. Having him home had been beyond wonderful, but they were sad he had to head back to the Northwest
Territories on Christmas morning. Even worse, Elizabeth was
worried about his safety as he went back to the wartime dan-
gers that awaited him.

Yet in the midst of those uncertain times, Elizabeth
decided to write in her journal because it always helped to
strengthen her: "I've been blessed to spend these last few days

with Jack. Tonight will be our best Christmas Eve ever ... until he has to leave again. It will be a challenge not to show my concerns about his safety, so I have to remember that God has a plan—and we have to trust it." She was buoyed once again by hope.

Have you ever experienced circumstances at Christmastime that distressed you or caused you sadness? Maybe this is your first holiday without a loved one. Or perhaps there are worries that are so overwhelming that you can hardly breathe.

As Elizabeth learned, you can choose to cling to the One who gives us hope. And you can follow her example because of one certain truth: God is faithful. He has promised to be with us, to guide our steps, and to comfort us. He has a plan for each of our lives. We might not like it at times. We might not even understand it. But we can always, *always* trust it.

And those who know Your name
will put their trust in You;
For You, LORD, have not forsaken
those who seek You.

PSALM 9:10 NKJV

Dear Lord, things seem a little hopeless this Christmas, and I need to see a way out. I like being in control, but these situations seem out of control. Please help me to cling to you. Help me to turn my burdens over to you. Thank you for always being faithful and for the comfort of your presence. Help me to trust you even though I don't know exactly how this is going to go. Help me to remember that your plan for me is always best. Amen.

THE GIFT OF YOUR HEART

* **Why should you put your trust in God?**
* **What are some circumstances in the past where God has proven trustworthy to you?**

CRANBERRY ORANGE RELISH

From the Kitchen of Heartie Carol McLeod

This recipe is from my maternal grandmother, Mary Gills Boyce Blew. Raised by nuns in an orphanage in Ottawa, Ontario, she was a little Irish woman who could dance a jig, light up a room, and soothe a child's heart. When I make this recipe every Thanksgiving and Christmas, I love knowing that my grandmother made this same recipe every year for 50 years. Then she gave it to my aunt who made it for family gatherings for the next 30 years ... and now it is my turn.

The family legend is that she was taught this recipe by the nuns who raised her. They made it every Christmas in the orphanage as long as they could find an orange and some cranberries. Back then they just used unflavored gelatin, but we have changed it through the years to use orange-flavored.

INGREDIENTS

1 bag of cranberries
1 orange
1/2 cup of orange juice
1 large box of orange-flavored gelatin dessert
1 1/2 cups of boiling water
1 cup of sugar

PREPARATION

Grind the cranberries well in a food processor or blender. Leave the skin on the orange, cut it into chunks, and then put it in the blender with the cranberries. Add the 1/2 cup of orange juice to the cranberries and oranges so that it isn't too thick.

Mix the gelatin, boiling water, and sugar together until the gelatin and sugar are thoroughly dissolved. Then gently fold in the cranberry and orange mixture. Stir together until well mixed. Put it in a pretty serving dish and place it in the refrigerator for at least twenty-four hours before serving.

A Prayer Bear
on the Tree

From Heartie Michelle Cox

When my youngest son was a little guy, I walked around the corner one evening and discovered Jason sitting on the stairs looking at the bear tree that I'd decorated in our foyer. I'll never forget his words that day, "A house just looks better with a Christmas tree in it."

I have to agree with him. There's something special about a room that's lit by the soft glow of Christmas lights. There's a coziness and a warmth that invites us to just sit there and enjoy it—and it's even better when we do that together as a family.

Christmas trees can range from fancy gold, to glistening white, to homespun like what the residents of Hope Valley decorated. I love them and usually put up four trees each year. Two of them go outside on our deck. I so enjoy looking out the glass doors in my kitchen and seeing the white lights glowing out there against the backdrop of the night.

Our main tree goes in the family room. It's my sentimental tree, filled with ornaments from mine and Paul's first Christmas together, handmade treasures our sons brought home from school, ornaments from friends, some we've bought on our trips, and ones that we've made with our grandchildren. I love decorating that tree each year. Each glass ball and bauble brings back sweet memories of times with our family, and even more precious memories are added each year as our entire family gathers one evening to decorate that tree.

The final Christmas tree goes in our foyer. Yes, the bear tree that my son enjoyed all those years ago. I use all the teddy bears my sons had when they were little, bears we've bought on family vacations, and bears to commemorate special events such as graduations and weddings.

There are stuffed ones, glass bear ornaments, wooden ones, and one very special one: a bear holding a tiny Bible. This is the one I take off the tree each year to show my grand-babies, because for seven long years of prayer, it looked like we wouldn't have grandchildren. Tucked behind that bear's little Bible is a small folded piece of paper that says, "Trusting God for a child for Jeremy and Lydia and for Tim and Lau-rel." And now six special bears hang on that tree—one for each precious grandchild that God has sent to our family. I love the sweet memories tucked on the limbs of that tree.

It doesn't matter what kind of tree you have, but make it special for your family. And remember that Christmas trees are a great reminder of the Light of the World who arrived in a humble stable one Christmas, the God who personally dec-orated a tree on Calvary so that we could receive the greatest gift ever given.

19

KEEP WATCH FOR THE WATCHERS

*T*he Christmas parade was a big hit in Hope Valley. It had taken many hands and countless hours of labor to pull it off. But when the townspeople saw the results, it was clear that everyone's hard work had paid off.

The schoolchildren were adorable as they marched beside the North Pole-themed float dressed in their elf outfits. Jack and Elizabeth—grand marshals of the parade—beamed as they rode through town. And miracle of miracles, even the all-volunteer band sounded good.

Hope Valley's citizens lined the street, talking with their

neighbors, waving as their friends passed by on the floats, and laughing as the children dove to grab the candy that was thrown to the crowd.

And all alone, Henry Gowen stood in the doorway of the jail, intently watching the proceedings with a wistful look on his face.

Sometimes we forget that people are watching us. They take in how we live our lives, the examples we set, and whether we are even aware of them. And the scary truth is that we might be the only example of forgiveness and generosity that they will ever see. Is there a Henry Gowen in your life that you know is watching you, perhaps even envious of the peace, joy, and contentment that you have?

Keep an eye open this Christmas for someone who has their eye on you. And remember to stay so close to God that when others look at you, they see Him instead.

Let your light so shine before men,
that they may see your good works
and glorify your Father in heaven.

MATTHEW 5:16 NKJV

*Dear Father, sometimes it frightens me to think that
others are watching me. I mess up so often and I don't
want to fail you or them. Remind me that my children are
watching my life and trying to be like me. Remind me that
co-workers, friends, and even people at the grocery store
are paying attention to how I live my life. Help them to
see you in me. Make me the kind of person whose life
will make them hungry for you. Amen.*

THE GIFT OF YOUR HEART

✳ How does it affect you to realize that other people are watching how you live each day?

✳ What steps can you take to be a good example of God's love?

CHICKEN PENNE PASTA

From the Kitchen of Heartie Michelle Cox

This is my most requested recipe. This one is an original and my family and friends love it so much that they ask for it whenever I throw a party or have a get-together at my house. It's especially great around Christmas because it can be assembled the day before and then baked right before serving—which means the mess will be out of the way before your guests arrive.

INGREDIENTS

- 2 cups penne pasta
- 2 cans cream of chicken soup
- 1 cup sour cream
- 2 cups cooked chicken breasts, diced
- 3 tablespoons margarine or butter
- 1/4 cup hot water
- 1 chicken bouillon cube
- 1 cup shredded cheddar cheese

PREPARATION

Cook the penne pasta according to the package directions; rinse and drain. Mix the cream of chicken soup and the sour cream; divide it in half. Add the diced chicken and the penne pasta to one half of the soup/sour cream mixture. Stir and set aside.

In a medium-sized saucepan, melt the margarine over medium heat until it's lightly browned. Watch this carefully. Once it gets to a certain point, it can burn quickly. Stir frequently and swirl the butter around in the pan to keep it moving so it won't scorch.

Heat the water and then add the bouillon cube, stirring until blended. Add the browned butter. Stir and then add it to the second half of the soup/sour cream mixture; blend. Spray a 13x9x2 casserole with cooking spray and then add the chicken and pasta mixture; spread evenly. Pour the soup/butter mixture over the top; spread evenly. Bake uncovered at 375 degrees for about 20–30 minutes or until bubbly. Add the cheese to the top and then put it back in the oven for about five minutes, or until the cheese is melted. (Tip: To cut down on the fat and calories, use reduced fat cream of chicken soup, fat free or light sour cream, reduce the butter to two tablespoons, and use a combination of ¾ cup fat free cheddar cheese mixed with ¼ cup regular cheddar cheese.)

OUR CHRISTMAS
URBAN PLUNGE

From Heartie Brian Bird

*F*or many years while we were living in Southern California, and as members of Saddleback Church, on the Sunday night before each Christmas, our family would join other like-hearted families from church in a late-night sojourn to the mean streets of Los Angeles.

The project was called "Jackets for Jesus" and was inspired by the idea that Joseph, and his very-much-in-labor fiancée Mary, were essentially homeless on that first Christmas. Without a little help from a compassionate innkeeper and some lonely shepherds, that night in Bethlehem would have been one cold, nightmarish ordeal. Which is pretty much what life is like for homeless families living on the streets of any big city today.

Our task was simple. For several weeks leading up to Christmas, we would collect new and donated jackets, socks, and shoes and fill backpacks with toiletries and other essentials. The brains of the operation was Eric Denton, a pastor from Riverside, California, who has dedicated himself to ministering to the poor and dispossessed on the streets of Los Angeles' "Skid Row" district every Sunday night for many years.

On the designated pre-Christmas-plunge Sunday night, we would get in vans at 9 p.m. and head to Skid Row, where thousands of homeless would be waiting, quietly and grate-fully, for our arrival. The line stretched for several blocks and the men, women, and children, would first be served a hot meal of turkey, stuffing, and yams. And then they would proceed down the line to receive their backpack, jackets, and other items of clothing.

I have heard over the years from some contrarians that hand-outs are bad for poor people. That they foster dependence and a lack of independence. That people should be encouraged to pick themselves up by their bootstraps and make something of their lives. What these arguments fail to recognize is that you have to have boots to have bootstraps. And that there are many complex reasons for poverty, including hard life circumstances and even mental illness.

The last time I checked Jesus' parable "The Good Samar-itan," it was the contrarians who wouldn't have anything to do with the injured traveler beaten by robbers and left for dead on the side of the road. But it was the Samaritan who stopped and cared for the man. Who went the extra mile. And he was the one honored by Jesus in the story.

That's what "Jackets for Jesus" is all about. And for many years, it was a transformational experience for my family. Amid the "Gimme, Gimme!" commercialism of Christmas, what an amazing lesson it was for my kids, on a cold December Sunday night, to stand across from less fortunate men, women, and kids, all with their own stories to tell. And to learn an import-ant truth: "There but for the grace of God, go I."

It's exactly the lesson of that night in the manger in Bethlehem.

20

CHRISTMAS
IN OUR HEARTS

J ack grunted as he hoisted the heavy trunk from the stage
coach as Lee and Rosemary arrived home from their honeymoon. Lee explained that Rosemary had gone Christmas
shopping every day while they were away. And her Christmas
planning didn't stop there.

When Lee returned home from work the following day,
he was stunned. Christmas decorations covered every surface
of their little row house. There was so much to take in that he
didn't know where to look next. Rosemary was in Christmas
mode, trying to make things perfect. It consumed her.

We laugh at Rosemary's antics, but do we really do any less in our modern lives? We rush around for weeks before the holidays. We make lists, send piles of Christmas cards, purchase and wrap gifts, and watch Yuletide movies 24-7. We bake and cook and host get-togethers with family and friends. We attend parties and church events. And the to-do list goes on and on as we push ourselves to exhaustion.

Are we missing what Christmas is all about? Are we ignoring the One whom the season is all about? Shouldn't we be pondering the story of His birth and how that changes the universe and our lives forever?

This year, sure, have fun and enjoy your celebrations. But more importantly, don't forget to make time to worship the Savior, to sing His praises, and to express your thanks for the most amazing gift ever given. Because that's when we'll truly have Christmas in our hearts.

Be still, and know that I am God;
I will be exalted among the nations,
I will be exalted in the earth!

PSALM 46:10 NKJV

*Dear Lord, Christmas is your birthday, and yet you often
get pushed aside in the midst of my other activities. Help
me to slow down my days—to be still—and to look for ways
that I can make you the focus of each day. Help me to learn
about you and hear from your heart. I want to worship
you—to give you the honor and praise that is due to you.
Thank you for your amazing gift. Don't ever let me take
that for granted. Amen.*

THE GIFT OF YOUR HEART

* **How do you sometimes push God to the sidelines in the midst of your Christmas activities?**

* **What can you do to make more time to worship God this Christmas?**

LYNETTE'S FAMILY FAVORITE MEATBALLS

From the Kitchen of Heartie Lynette Eason

INGREDIENTS

- 1 lb. ground beef
- 1 egg
- 2 cups bread crumbs
- 1/3 cup milk
- 1 teaspoon salt
- 1/4 teaspoon pepper
- 1 pkg. brown gravy mix
- 1 1/4 cups water

PREPARATION

Mix the ground beef, egg, bread crumbs, milk, salt, and pepper together with your hands until everything is blended. Make into medium size meatballs. Bake at 425 degrees for 20 minutes.

Mix the gravy mix and water together. Put the meatballs into a big pot and pour the gravy over them. Let them simmer for 15–20 minutes. Place into a pretty serving dish and enjoy. (Tip: Lynette says these can be made gluten-free by purchasing gluten-free bread crumbs and brown gravy mix.)

CHRISTMAS PRAYER TRADITIONS

From Heartie Sonya Williams

*O*n each night of December leading up to Christmas Day, my family gathers in the living room all decorated with lights and red and gold, and just before going to bed, we read the Christmas cards we've received that day, along with our Christmas story advent calendar. We include these family, friends, and loved ones in our family prayer and devotion time and pray for them, their specific needs, and their families.

CHRISTMAS PRAYERS THROUGHOUT THE YEAR

From Heartie Michelle Cox

*T*he Cox family takes Sonya's idea one step further. We hang onto the Christmas cards we receive, and through-out the year, we choose one family each week and we pray for them. At the beginning of the week, we send a message and tell them we're praying for them and ask if they have any special requests. This prayer time has become as much a blessing to us as it is to the family we're praying for, and as the year goes by, it's often clear that those prayers couldn't arrive at a more perfect time. Clearly, God's timing is always better than ours.

෨෨

An Antique Candlestick

From Heartie Charlotte Adelsperger

O n Christmas Eve, our grandchildren come with their parents to our home. To begin our celebration, I always point them to a 140-year-old pewter candlestick that displays a tall red candle. The children know the history. The seven-inch candlestick first belonged to my great-great-grandmother, who lived around the time of Abraham Lincoln. It was passed down to each successive generation, and now to me. Every person who owned it believed that Jesus is the Light of the World. After a prayer together, the children light the candle. It glows and flickers all evening in our living room as we open presents and celebrate Christ's birth.

A PICNIC AT CHRISTMAS

From Heartie Christi Miller

*E*very year since our girls were little, we've set aside time once or twice during the holiday season to have a picnic by the Christmas tree. We gather up lots of favorite snacks and treats—some given to us by others, and some that we've made together. We spread a blanket on the floor and enjoy our picnic while watching Christmas favorites like *Rudolph* or *Veggie Tales*. Our girls are tweens and teens now, but we still cherish the memories of this special tradition.

ORNAMENTS FOR GENERATIONS

From Heartie Carrie Austin

*O*ur family has passed on a tradition to our church family. My girls and I make about sixty Christmas ornaments for the youth in our church every year. My hope is that the children of our church will look back on those ornaments someday and remember they were made and given with love—and that they will have the desire to carry on this tradition in their own families.

ᏣᎦ *21* ᏣᎦ

ANTICIPATION

*T*he citizens of Hope Valley prepared their little town for Christmas with contagious excitement. Folks laughed together as they wound red ribbons around the posts of all the porches, and hung wreaths and greenery from the rails. A tree was carefully chosen and set up in the middle of town and decorated with homemade ornaments. The final touch of snow drifts and children throwing snowballs made it picture perfect. Sheriff Bill Avery even made his famous eggnog. Miss Thatcher and the children decorated the schoolhouse with red and green paper garlands. They made gingerbread houses, and planned some special holiday activities. Christmas was coming and the entire town was abuzz with anticipation.

For us today, Christmas can be beautiful and blessed and a big blast of fun. And there is nothing wrong with that sense of anticipation of making it an awesome experience. But we should also be mindful of an important distinction: Have you ever looked forward to spending time together with God with that kind of excitement, wonder, and anticipation?

God tells us that if we'll just look for Him, we'll find Him. And that happens when we read His Word, spend time in prayer, and listen for His voice. The God of the universe wants to be close to us. He wants to know our hearts. And this special time of the year is the perfect time to come to Him with fresh, new anticipation as we seek to know *His* heart.

And you will seek Me and find Me,
when you search for Me with all your heart.
JEREMIAH 29:13 NKJV

*Dear Father, it amazes me that you want to spend time with
me. I want to learn your heart. I want a deep, meaningful
relationship with you. Light a fire of excitement in my heart
for you and for your truth in the scriptures. Help me to
anticipate our times together and mold me into what you
desire for me. Help me to seek you all the days of my life,
and help others to see you in me. Amen.*

THE GIFT OF YOUR HEART

* **How can you learn to know God's heart?**
* **Why should you look forward with anticipation
when it comes to spending time with Him?**

MAMA'S CHOCOLATE GRAVY

From the Kitchen of Heartie Tenesia Berry

I grew up in a small coal mining town in southwest Virginia. Christmas was always a special time because we knew there'd be new toys, clothes, and an orange in our stocking.

One of the things that mom used to make—that assured us that Christmas had arrived—was chocolate gravy. I know that may sound unusual to some at first but you really need to give it a try. It's a sweet, almost dessert-type dish that we'd eat for breakfast, adding a little bit of butter and biscuits. I typed the recipe just as my mom gave it to me. Like many good cooks, you'll notice there aren't precise measurements for all the ingredients, but you'll discover that's okay.

INGREDIENTS

4–6 tablespoons of Hershey's cocoa (has to be from the old fashioned square can)

6–8 tablespoons of sugar

Self-rising flour (to thicken), usually 1–2 tablespoons

1 can sweetened condensed milk

1–2 cups of boiling water

Butter, to taste

PREPARATION

Mix the cocoa, sugar, and flour in a medium-sized pan. Add the sweetened condensed milk slowly, stirring well to get a smooth consistency.

Boil the water in a pan. Add the chocolate mixture to the boiling water and stir until it thickens. This should only take a few minutes. Spoon a puddle of chocolate onto your plate, and then add butter (to taste). Serve with biscuits.

SAVE THE BEST
FOR LAST

From Heartie Brian Bird

*A*s a writer and storyteller, I am wired for escalation. In the scenes I write, I'm always striving to build the suspense to a culmination. Conflict is supposed to rise, not peter out. The story climax is always near the end, not the beginning. In a joke, you save the punchline for last. That's how we all are accustomed to hearing stories, right?

Well, it's with this conundrum that I approach Christmas morning each year. Patty, my bride of four decades, and I always have the same debate every Yuletide. Do we open the "Santa" gifts first or last? In our house, the Santa gifts are the premium loot. The best gifts. The pearl of great price gifts. Our five kids, not so young anymore, and some even with their own spouses now, are fairly agnostic on the issue.

Patty feels the Santa gifts should be the first to fall. They should accompany the chock-full stockings on the fireplace hearth along with the half-consumed Santa glass of milk and plate of cookies. They should just be sitting there because, well, that's Mr. Claus' way of doing things. And then it's all downhill after that. I can imagine a scenario where the youngsters don't even crack open their final gifts. Just not worth the effort. Might as well be reindeer droppings. Sure, that scenario props up the Santa legacy, but it's bust in terms of storytelling.

The writer in me wants escalation. I want to start with lame gifts first (lame, as in items of underclothing or foot-sheathing). And then we build the suspense by gradually opening up the sweeter booty—until *BOOM*—the ultimate Christmas present!

Isn't my method just so much more satisfying? Like seeing a movie or a certain television show that makes its long-suffering fans wait for five seasons for a wedding of its two favorite characters. Delicious anticipation by saving the best for last.

⚜ 22 ⚜

SOMETIMES WE JUST NEED TO LOOK BACK

*T*he traveling peddler, Sam, seemed to have something on his wagon for just about everyone in Hope Valley. One day, as Pastor Frank passed by, he looked a little down, and Sam inquired about whether he needed a Bible. After all, "A man of God can always use a Bible."

Frank replied that he had plenty of Bibles. But then Sam mentioned he'd gotten one from Granville Penitentiary that Frank might like. The pastor had served time at Granville, and when he looked at the Bible, he saw the Saint Francis prayer handwritten in the back.

Emotion colored Frank's voice: "This was my Bible." Sam said that what he'd learned from that Bible must have changed a lot of lives, and that perhaps more could be changed.

Sometimes we just need to look back at how far God has brought us from our past mistakes and challenges in order to realize how faithful He is. He's forgiven us and promised to be with us and guide us. Yet it's so easy to forget that we can depend on Him when new challenges come. He is the God who will *always* be with us. The God who loves us more than His own life.

Christmas is a perfect time to remember His faithfulness in the past, so that we can be confident today, and know just how much He will love and care for us tomorrow, and every day for the rest of our lives.

Remember the things I have done in the past.
For I alone am God! I am God,
and there is none like me.

ISAIAH 46:9 NLT

*Dear Father, you have always been so faithful to me—and
yet whenever I encounter problems, I forget to trust you.
Help me to remember what you've done for me. Remind me
of your faithfulness in the past so that I can trust you in the
future. You've been faithful—and I want to be faithful to
you, so that others will see what you've done for me. Amen.*

THE GIFT OF YOUR HEART

* **Why do you so often forget that God is faithful?**
* **Why should you share your stories of God's
  faithfulness with your family and friends?**

PEPPERMINT CREAM CHEESE FROSTING

From the Kitchen of Heartie Dee Dee Baxter Parker

INGREDIENTS

24 chocolate cupcakes (from your favorite homemade recipe
   or a Swiss chocolate cake mix)
8 oz. cream cheese, softened
1 stick (1/2 cup) butter, softened
1 box powdered sugar
1 teaspoon vanilla
1/8 teaspoon of red food coloring
54 peppermints, divided

PREPARATION

Put the softened cream cheese and butter in a large mixing bowl.
Beat with an electric mixer until the mixture is light and fluffy. Add
the powdered sugar slowly ... unless you like clouds of sugar dust in
your face. Blend well and then add the vanilla. Add 1/8 teaspoon of
red food coloring. Blend and then keep adding food coloring in small
increments until you reach the desired color.

Unwrap twelve of the peppermints and place them in a freezer-
type bag. Use the flat side of a meat mallet (or something similar) to
break the peppermint into small pieces. (Kids love this part. Just be
careful of little hands.) Stir into the cream cheese mixture.

Frost the cupcakes. Unwrap eighteen more peppermints and crush
them in a freezer-type bag. Pour the pieces onto a small plate and then
roll the edges of the cupcakes in the peppermint bits.

Unwrap the final 24 pieces of peppermint and stand one up on
top of each cupcake for a garnish.

CHRISTMAS HOPE
IN A PAIR OF SHOES

From Heartie Bernadette Kozak

*T*he year was 1967. As Christmas neared, my mother was eight months pregnant with her fifth child. The rest of us children were 12, 10 (me), 9, and 5. Besides the pregnancy, my mother had become ill, and she was so depressed that winter that all the Christmas preparations had stopped dead in their tracks. My father had done all he could do tending to my mother. We tried to pick up the pieces, but Christmas Eve day arrived and everything seemed so bleak.

In years past, my parents had always made a big deal of Christmas. Our father didn't make a lot of money, but it wasn't about the money. It was about the pomp and circumstances surrounding the Christ child.

Back during the good times, they'd bought a large manger set which was contained in a box that opened like the Bible. Baby Jesus was a beautiful doll that was large enough to hold. When we were younger, when we did good deeds, we could add straw to His manger to soften His bed. My five-year-old brother, Mark, was still doing that in 1967.

This year, Justin, the oldest, rallied all the sibling troops. We decided to lay out our best clothes for the Christmas Day church service and discovered that Mark's dress shoes were too small. So we set out on foot to the mall before it closed, hoping to find him new ones. We felt like we could save the day if we met our goal to all be dressed up for the service. It would not work out if Mark wore sneakers with his suit!

Since it was nearly supper time, the mall was almost empty. Downstairs in Newberry's, we looked at the rack of shoes for boys. The shelves were nearly bare. Nothing fit, and we were heartbroken.

Then I noticed a rack farther down, near the aisle. We could see one lone pair of shoes. We walked over and discovered that they were boys' dress shoes … and they were Mark's exact size.

We hopped around and whooped for joy. In our young minds, Jesus was paying Mark back for all the straw he'd put in His manger—straw that Mark had earned by doing good things for others.

My mother was still depressed, my father was still trying to help her, and things didn't really get better—except in our hearts. We were convinced that Jesus was there in Newberry's that Christmas Eve, helping us get ready to visit Him the next morning.

No, our circumstances hadn't changed, but the memory of that special Christmas moment—and God's unexpected provision for four little children as they hunted for hope and a pair of shoes—is one that we'll never forget.

23

ARE YOU THE ONE HE LEAVES THE NINETY-NINE TO FIND?

*P*eddler Sam was touched by Pastor Frank's concern for Nancy Tucker and her son, Harper, who folks hadn't seen for a few days. But Frank didn't know where to begin looking for them. Sam gently reminded Frank that a star led the wise men to Bethlehem—his hint that God would lead Frank.

God didn't send a star to Pastor Frank, but He did send a clue as to where Nancy might have gone following the death of her husband. Frank's heart was touched with compassion for her and Harper, so he set out to search for them. He didn't want them to be alone for Christmas, and in his heart, he knew that staying in Hope Valley was the right decision for them.

He went after them because he cared, and he searched until he found them.

Isn't that just what God always does for us when we stray from Him? As Luke chapter 15 teaches, the good shepherd is not afraid to leave his ninety-nine other sheep in order to go search for the one sheep that is lost.

It's the same way with us. God never abandons us, never stops searching for us, and is always preparing the way home. He loves us that much. Are you the lost sheep He's searching for today? Don't run from Him. Run *to* Him—and there will be great rejoicing as the Shepherd gathers you into the safety of His loving arms.

"What man of you, having a hundred sheep,
if he loses one of them, does not leave the ninety-nine
in the wilderness, and go after the one which is lost
until he finds it? And when he has found it,
he lays it on his shoulders, rejoicing."

LUKE 15:4–5 NKJV

*Dear God, it boggles my mind that you never stop
searching for me because you love me so much. Thank you
for caring enough to do that, for never giving up on me until
I'm back with you. Help me not to wander from you, and
to always look for you whenever I take a step that might
inadvertently lead me away. And please help me to
remember to always stay close to you. Amen.*

THE GIFT OF YOUR HEART

* **Who are some friends or family members you could "search" for today to tell them about God?**

* **Why is it easy to wander away from God and how can you do a better job of staying close to Him?**

TROPICAL SPREAD WITH CINNAMON TORTILLA CHIPS

From the Kitchen of Bruce Brown

Michelle's note: This is one of my favorite things to serve when family and friends come over—and it always gets rave reviews. Bruce Brown (of Bruce's Fabulous Foods in Marion, North Carolina) does food segments on our local television station, and this is one of the recipes that he prepared on there. I was so thrilled that he gave permission for me to share it with you, and I have no doubts that it will become a favorite at your house as well.

INGREDIENTS

16 oz. cream cheese, softened

1/2 cup granulated sugar

1/2 teaspoon vanilla

1/2 cup shredded coconut

11 oz. can mandarin oranges, drained

8 oz. can of crushed pineapple, drained

Maraschino cherries

Cinnamon Sugar Tortilla Chips

10 (10-inch) flour tortilla chips

Butter flavored cooking spray

2 cups cinnamon sugar

PREPARATION

Whip the cream cheese, sugar, and vanilla; add the coconut. Drain the mandarin oranges and pineapple and add them to the cream cheese mixture. Garnish with maraschino cherries. Serve with cinnamon sugar tortilla chips.

To make the chips, preheat the oven to 350 degrees. Spray one side of each flour tortilla with cooking spray. Cut into wedges and arrange in a single layer on a large cookie sheet. Sprinkle the wedges with the cinnamon sugar. Spray again with the butter-flavored cooking spray. Bake for about 4–8 minutes or until the chips are crisp. Repeat with the remaining tortilla chips. Allow to cool about 15 minutes before serving. (Tip: In a hurry? You can buy cinnamon sugar pita chips. And if you're making your own from this recipe, an easy way to cut the wedges is to use a pizza cutter. Also, I [Michelle] use 1/2 teaspoon of coconut extract instead of the 1/2 teaspoon of vanilla in the tropical cream cheese spread.)

MOTHER'S CHRISTMAS TABLECLOTH

From Heartie Linda Gilden

I'd always loved the tradition of putting my mother's Christmas tablecloth on the dining room table in early December. She'd cross-stitched it when I was a little girl as I sat by her side. I always said I wanted to have a tablecloth just like that when I grew up.

Mother found a similar Christmas tablecloth kit in a sewing store in New England and purchased two of them—one for me and one for my sister. My sister completed hers soon after Mother gave them to us. I put mine in the closet and planned to finish it in plenty of time for Christmas.

In late October, I decided I should start cross-stitching, but despite searching for months, my tablecloth kit was nowhere to be found.

And now, Christmas Eve had arrived with the tablecloth still unfinished. My mother and sister bounced with excitement as they handed me a present, "Open this one first!"

The family gathered around as I slowly opened the mystery package. I stared in disbelief. There was my tablecloth—totally finished for me with every cross perfectly stitched. And now when I use it each Christmas, it's extra special, because every stitch was made with love.

A SPECIAL CHRISTMAS
MEMORY

From Heartie Lynda Foote

My husband and I created our family through international adoption. Our son came home on a plane from Korea as an infant. We brought his sister home from Russia six and a half years later when she had just turned five. She arrived in October and wasn't speaking English yet, so she had a crazy holiday season that year. First we had Halloween, then her half-sister's wedding, then Thanksgiving, and finally Christmas. It seemed like it was all just one big party.

A couple of years before, friends had introduced my son to a St. Nicholas Eve tradition. We put shoes by our fireplace on December 5 in anticipation of a treat from St. Nick. Our little Russian princess dutifully copied her brother's lead without having a clue what to expect. The next morning as she searched in her shoe, she was delighted to find a new ornament in one, while the other was filled with candy. But she caught on fast. We found her snow boots by the fireplace that night.

24

THE GREATEST STORY
EVER TOLD

By Jordan Blackstone

"*A*nd the glory of the Lord shone round about them, and they were sore afraid ..." Elizabeth Thatcher read from the book of Luke to the townsfolk gathered for the nativity play.

Dressed in angel and shepherd costumes, the children continued quoting the familiar verses as the Christmas story was told. Wise men in bathrobes, fake beards, and gold crowns stood beside the manger where Mary and Joseph gazed at baby Jesus.

Pastor Frank perfectly summed up the evening, "It's hard to follow the greatest story ever told, so I won't even try—but I do want to remind everyone that the greatest gift we receive is God's love. The greatest gift that we give is the love we have for one another."

His words carry a powerful message for all of us. There's no greater story than the birth of that baby in Bethlehem. God's love is a priceless gift—and He doesn't want us to keep that news to ourselves. The story of His grace, love, and mercy is one that everyone needs to hear—a story that will change lives, provide hope, and comfort hearts. That is the great take-away of Christmas for all of us: God first loved us … so that in turn we can love each other.

When's the last time you shared God's love story with someone you love? This Christmas would be a perfect time to start telling that news to everyone who needs to hear it.

Sing to the LORD, bless His name;
proclaim the good news of His salvation from
day to day. Declare His glory among the nations,
His wonders among all peoples.

PSALM 96:2–3 NKJV

*Dear God, thank you for the gift of your Son on that
Christmas so long ago. That truly is the greatest story ever
told—yet I often keep that news to myself as if it were my own
little secret. Give me courage and boldness to tell others about
your love and forgiveness. Remind me that I'm to love others
as you have loved me. Amen.*

THE GIFT OF YOUR HEART

* Why are you so often hesitant about telling
  others of God's love?

* God loves us even though we don't deserve it.
  How can you carry that into your relationships
  with others?

WHITE CHOCOLATE STRAWBERRY STICKS

From the Kitchen of Heartie Karen Whiting

INGREDIENTS

Bottom Blondie Layer

- 1/2 cup sugar
- 1/4 cup brown sugar
- 1/2 cup butter
- 1 egg
- 1/2 teaspoon vanilla
- 1 1/4 cups all-purpose flour
- 1 teaspoon baking soda

Middle Strawberry Cream Cheese Layer

- 2 tablespoons butter, melted
- 2 oz. cream cheese, softened
- 1 teaspoon strawberry flavoring
- Red food coloring (a few drops)
- 2 cups powdered sugar

Top Chocolate Layer

- 12 oz. white chocolate chips

PREPARATION

For the bottom blondie layer, preheat the oven to 375 degrees. Cream the sugar, the brown sugar, and the butter together. Add the egg and the 1/2 teaspoon of vanilla; mix until blended. Add the flour and the teaspoon of baking soda. Stir until well mixed. Pour into a greased 11x7 pan. Bake for about 15–18 minutes, or until a toothpick inserted in the center comes out clean. Cool, and then add the strawberry cream cheese layer.

For the middle strawberry cream cheese layer, mix two tablespoons of melted butter, 2 oz. of softened cream cheese, 1 teaspoon of strawberry flavoring, a few drops of red food coloring, and 2 cups of powdered sugar until smooth. Spread this onto the cooled bottom layer. Let it harden.

Melt the 12 oz. of white chocolate chips in the microwave (in 30-second increments until melted) and spread on the top. Let the white chocolate cool. Cut into thin sticks (1/2 inch by 3 inches). (Tip: To keep the white chocolate from cracking and breaking as you cut this, you might want to cut it before the white chocolate has set up completely.)

PASSING DOWN OUR CHRISTMAS HEIRLOOMS

From Heartie Michelle Cox

I am quite sentimental, so I especially love traditions. One of ours began the year our first son was born. We decided we'd buy an ornament each year for Jeremy (we did the same when Tim and Jason were born), and then we'd wrap the ornaments up as a gift when they got married. That sounded so simple, but years later when that time came, it sure was hard to give those ornaments away.

I cried as I packed the box. It was amazing how so many memories were attached to those ornaments—the fun of picking them out together, little hands placing them on the limbs, and sitting around the tree enjoying them together as a family.

I wasn't the only one who wiped tears away. All three of our sons cried at their household showers when they opened their boxes of ornaments, and their daddy did as well. But it's always so sweet to see those familiar ornaments hanging on their Christmas trees now that our boys are grown and have families of their own.

That's been a special tradition for all of us, and we've now carried that on to our grandchildren—except we make our ornaments together each year because I want them to have Christmas memories of fun times with Grandmama and with their cousins. I suspect their parents will also have a hard time giving those ornaments to them when they get married.

I've loved our ornaments, but my favorite traditions arrive on Christmas Eve. That's when our family opens our gifts. But, first, we turn the focus to the real reason for the season.

We begin by reading the Christmas story together from Luke 2:1–16. Now that we have grandchildren, we sit the manger set on the floor in the middle of the room, and each child takes one or two of the figurines. As the story is read, when it comes to their part, they place Mary and Joseph, or the sheep or angel into place in the stable. I love watching those sweet little faces as they take part in the greatest story ever told.

And then we all pray together as a family, each person taking a turn to thank God for His amazing gift to us and for all the things He's blessed us with that year. I don't have words to describe how precious that is.

With six little ones, opening gifts is a time filled with excitement, mayhem, and mounds of wrapping paper. I love it. And then we polish off the evening with a cake for Jesus, and sing "Happy Birthday" to Him.

I'm so glad we've had these traditions—these family Christmas heirlooms—and I hope my children and grandchildren will carry them on to future generations.

What kind of traditions have you established for *your* family?

25

AFTER CHRISTMAS

*T*he citizens of Hope Valley worked hard to make their town festive for Christmas. Their little community took on such charm it looked like something from a postcard. There were plenty of eager volunteers to hang wreaths and decorate the tree in the middle of town.

But what about after Christmas? That's a different story, in Hope Valley and in our lives. Volunteers are usually in short supply when it comes to un-decorating and packing away the holiday boxes. But as a new year beckons, every December 26 is always time to move on.

The festivities are wonderful—a gift from God. But there comes a time when we need to put away the frivolous, and figure out how to be faithful when the lights aren't flickering and the egg nog isn't flowing—because the purpose of Christmas isn't just a one-day event—it's for eternity.

What if we eagerly planned for *after* Christmas and how to live more godly lives in the coming year? What if we decorated our hearts with a new love for Him and others? What if we wrapped ourselves in gifts of service? What if we worshipped Him with joy all the time?

Let's take the meaning of Christmas with us into the new year. Let's make this the year we draw closer to Him, where we listen for His whispers, where we make ourselves available for whatever He asks—and where we share His story with a world that desperately needs to hear it.

Only fear the LORD and serve him faithfully
with all your heart. For consider what
great things he has done for you.

I SAMUEL 12:24 ESV

*Dear Lord, this is the day we commemorate your birth,
but I'm the one who received the best gift. That you gave
your Son for us is beyond my comprehension. I know I
can never repay you, but I want my life to daily show my
gratitude. As the new year approaches, help me to live for
you like never before. Remind me that planning for after
Christmas is just as important because the message of
your gift to us matters for eternity. Help me to be
faithful all the days of my life. Amen.*

THE GIFT OF YOUR HEART

* We make extensive plans for Christmas, but we
  rarely plan for *after* Christmas. What plans do
  you want to make spiritually for the upcoming
  year?

* Why does the gift of God's Son matter for
  eternity?

AUNT FLORENCE'S EGG DISH

From the Kitchen of Heartie Patty Bird

On Christmas morning I always make a big breakfast—and that includes this egg dish that Brian's Aunt Florence gave me more than thirty years ago. (By the way, Florence on *When Calls the Heart* was named after our Aunt Florence.)

INGREDIENTS

4 cups of white bread, cubed
1 pkg. of regular sausage, cooked and crumbled
2 cups shredded sharp cheddar cheese
1/2 cup sliced mushrooms (optional)
10 eggs, slightly beaten
4 cups whole milk
1 teaspoon dry mustard (if you don't have dry mustard, I have used regular mustard and it works)
1 teaspoon salt
1/4 teaspoon onion powder
fresh pepper, to taste
1 can cream of mushroom soup

PREPARATION

Cut the bread into cubes (without crust) and then place the bread on the bottom of a 13x9x2 pan that's been coated with cooking spray. Top with the crumbled cooked sausage and the cheese. Add the sliced mushrooms if desired. Combine the slightly beaten eggs, the milk, dry mustard, salt, onion powder, and pepper.

Mix well and then pour the mixture evenly over the bread. Cover the casserole dish and chill overnight. Right before baking, spread one can of mushroom soup on top. Bake at 325-350 degrees for one hour.

Every Day
Is Christmas

From Heartie Brian Bird

O ne spring morning when I was a boy, I received a lesson in faith in the bathroom mirror from my maternal grandpa, Clarence Benson. My grandparents had been staying with us, so that Grandpa, a lifelong handyman, could help us with some home improvement projects.

It was early, and I woke up to the sound of the Christmas hymn "Oh, Holy Night" being hummed quietly. It made me curious since it was probably closer to Easter than it was to Christmas. I followed the sound of his song to the open bathroom door where I saw Grandpa shaving in front of the mirror.

He invited me in for a chat, and we talked a while about what project he was going to be taking on that day—sanding and painting one of our bedrooms. He was that kind of grandfather. A jack of all trades who had worked with his hands all his life, helping build dams, bridges, prisons, and houses—back before there were unions, safety rules, and limits on how hard you could work a man on construction sites. He had plenty of scars from all the ways strong-shouldered men could be taken advantage of back in the day. But he was also just as soft as he was tough, a gentle soul who was equally as skilled grooming a horse as he was swinging a hammer.

He was always a favorite with his grandkids. Every time we would greet him, he would swallow up our little hands in his big calloused mitts, and when he finally let go, there would always be a quarter in our hands. A silver dollar in good years.

That morning, with the smell of Barbasol in the air, and that scraping of a straight-edge razor blade on old-man stubble, I asked him why he was singing a Christmas carol in the middle of March. His reflection looked at me, smiled, and said, "Because, Brian, every day is Christmas."

I didn't really get it back then. But I do now. Every day is an opportunity to celebrate life, to give a gift to someone who needs one—because that's what the Creator of the cosmos did for us that first Christmas ... and every day since. In Romans 12:10, we are encouraged to "be devoted to one another in love" and to "honor one another above yourselves" (NIV). And that's what Grandpa Benson was trying to tell me. All the time ... not just on December 25. So don't be surprised if the next time I shake your hand, you find a quarter in your palm!

THE CHRISTMAS STORY

Luke 2:1–16 (KJV)

*A*nd it came to pass in those days, that there went out a decree from Caesar Augustus that all the world should be taxed.

(And this taxing was first made when Cyrenius was governor of Syria.)

And all went to be taxed, every one into his own city.

And Joseph also went up from Galilee, out of the city of Nazareth, into Judaea, unto the city of David, which is called Bethlehem; (because he was of the house and lineage of David:)

To be taxed with Mary his espoused wife, being great with child.

And so it was, that, while they were there, the days were accomplished that she should be delivered.

And she brought forth her firstborn son, and wrapped him in swaddling clothes, and laid him in a manger; because there was no room for them in the inn.

And there were in the same country shepherds abiding in the field, keeping watch over their flock by night.

And, lo, the angel of the Lord came upon them, and the glory of the Lord shone round about them: and they were sore afraid.

And the angel said unto them, Fear not: for, behold, I bring you good tidings of great joy, which shall be to all people.

For unto you is born this day in the city of David a Saviour, which is Christ the Lord.

And this shall be a sign unto you; Ye shall find the babe wrapped in swaddling clothes, lying in a manger.

And suddenly there was with the angel a multitude of the heavenly host praising God, and saying,

Glory to God in the highest, and on earth peace, good will toward men.

And it came to pass, as the angels were gone away from them into heaven, the shepherds said one to another, Let us now go even unto Bethlehem, and see this thing which is come to pass, which the Lord hath made known unto us.

And they came with haste, and found Mary, and Joseph, and the babe lying in a manger.

ACKNOWLEDGMENTS

*T*his book wouldn't have happened without the awesome team that made it a reality. We're grateful to our publisher, Carlton Garborg, for his friendship and guidance. Many thanks to David Sluka, Michelle Winger, Bill Watkins, Andy Kauth, and the rest of the editorial and sales team at BroadStreet Publishing. You make the process a pleasure.

Thank you to the amazing promotion and marketing team—Suzanne Niles, Jackie Medina, Sarah Peterson, Sarah LeVoir, and Lindsey Tradup. And thank you to Chris Garborg for making our books so beautiful.

We're grateful to Dee Dee Parker for loaning props to use for the recipe pictures and for her assistance in staging photos, and to Terenia Autrey for her help with photograph editing. (We'll feature those photos on social media and on our website at WhenGodCallstheHeart.com.) And thank you to Patty Bird and Lorraine Sherlin for their recipe help.

To all the people at Motion Picture Corporation of America and Believe Pictures, the production companies behind *When Calls the Heart*, thank you for the use of images and storylines. Specifically, Executive Producers Brad Krevoy, Eric Jarboe, and Michael Landon, Jr., and producers Vicki Sotheran and Greg Malcolm, along with five seasons of television's best writers.

Thanks also to the Hallmark Channel, specifically Chief Executive Officer Bill Abbott and Executive Vice President Michelle Vicary, for making a family and faith series at a time when no other TV network is paying attention to a vastly underserved audience.

Thank you to Janette Oke for your encouragement, your prayers, and for giving us such fantastic characters and stories to glean from. We love you. And thanks to the brilliant author Beverly Lewis for her beautiful, generous foreword to this devotional, and to those who graciously wrote endorsements for our book.

We're grateful to our prayer team. You're the strength behind what we do. We appreciate your faithfulness to pray for us and our work.

Thank you to our wonderful agent, Tamela Hancock Murray. Your prayers and advice mean the world to us.

We're grateful to Jordan Blackstone for the use of five of her gorgeous paintings in our book. Visit her website at imaginethatjbphotography.com for more delightful scenes from Hope Valley.

The two of us are truly blessed with the best spouses on the planet. Thank you to Patty Bird and to Paul Cox for their encouragement, help, support, and love. There's no way we could do what we do without them.

Most of all, we want to thank God who took a simple conversation over pizza and turned that into a series of books. We're humbled that He lets us be part of this journey.

Finally, thanks to the "Hearties"—the best fan community in all the world. There are no words to express how much we love and appreciate you. Your kindness, love, and support for our books, and for the values contained in *When Calls the Heart* and *When God Calls the Heart*, have touched our hearts immensely.

We prayed for you as we worked on *When God Calls the Heart at Christmas*, and we hope it will bless you and your family.

Merry Christmas from our homes to yours!

ABOUT THE AUTHORS

BRIAN BIRD

Brian Bird is Executive Producer and Co-Creator of the Hallmark Channel original series *When Calls the Heart*. In his three decades in Hollywood, he has written or produced two dozen films, including most recently, *The Case for Christ, Captive,* and *Not Easily Broken*, and more than 250 episodes of such shows as *Touched by An Angel, Step by Step,* and *Evening Shade*.

His films have garnered awards from the New York Independent Film Festival, New York Festivals, Heartland Film Festival, the Movieguide® Awards, the Telly Awards, and the Christopher Awards.

He has spoken widely on the intersection of the arts and the church, and his professional blog, brianbird.net, serves as a lively exchange in the best practices of storytelling. Beyond Bird's professional achievements, he considers his top productions to date his thirty-seven-year marriage to his wife, Patty, and his five children.

MICHELLE COX

Known for her "encouragement with a Southern drawl," Michelle Cox is a speaker and an award-winning, best-selling author. She is a member of the blog team for *Guideposts*, and her "Life with a Southern Grandmother" column runs twice each week at guideposts.org.

She has written for Focus on the Family, FoxNews.com, Christian Cinema, *WHOA Magazine for Women, Leading Hearts Magazine*, and the website of Fox News Radio Host Todd Starnes. Michelle is the creator of the Just 18 Summers® brand of parenting products and resources and has been a guest on numerous television and radio programs, including *Home & Family, Hannity*, and *Focus on the Family*. She and her husband, Paul, have been married for forty-four years, have three sons, three lovely daughters-in-law, and six perfect grandchildren.

Connect with Michelle at just18summers.com, on Twitter @MichelleInspire, and on Facebook at facebook.com/MichelleCoxInspirations.

Additional information about the *When God Calls the Heart* series of books and products can be found at WhenGodCallstheHeart.com.

WHEN GOD CALLS
the HEART *at* CHRISTMAS

KEEPSAKE JOURNAL

*F*ollow your heart to Hope Valley. Inspired by best-selling author Janette Oke and the Hallmark Channel original TV series *When Calls the Heart*, this inspirational journal is designed as a companion to the *When God Calls the Heart at Christmas* devotional. It will give you a place to keep those wonderful Christmas memories as you celebrate faith, family, friends, and the most meaningful Yuletide traditions.

Wrapped in exquisite faux leather, this elegant journal features high-quality paper with encouraging quotes.

Reflect on the beauty of God, delight in the knowledge of his love for you, and express your thoughts in the space provided.

ISBN 978-1-4245-5730-1
5x8 Faux Leather
160 pages
$16.99